CRETACEA & OTHER STORIES

CRETACEA

&

OTHER STORIES FROM THE BADLANDS

BY

MARTIN WEST

ANVIL PRESS / 2016

Anvil Press Publishers Inc.
P.O. Box 3008, Main Post Office
Vancouver, B.C. V6B 3X5 CANADA
www.anvilpress.com

Library and Archives Canada Cataloguing in Publication

West, Martin, 1959-, author
    Cretacea & other stories from the Badlands / Martin West.

ISBN 978-1-77214-049-1 (paperback)

    I. Title.

PS8645.E75C74 2016   C813'.6   C2016-903504-2

Printed and bound in Canada
Cover design by Rayola Graphic
Cover photo by the author
Interior by HeimatHouse
Represented in Canada by the Publishers Group Canada
Distributed by Raincoast Books

The publisher gratefully acknowledges the financial assistance of the Canada
Council for the Arts, the Canada Book Fund, and the Province of British Columbia
through the B.C. Arts Council and the Book Publishing Tax Credit.

CONTENTS

NOT A BAD MAN

MY UNCLE DALE wasn't an evil man, or even mean or bad looking. In fact, he wasn't really my uncle at all. He was my mother's cousin and so I'm not sure what that made him. But when he drove his rusted pickup truck down the sage-lined streets of Drumheller with one hand on my shoulder and the other on the horn, everyone probably thought those malicious things were true. All they saw was a dirty vagrant in stained coveralls drinking a beer and roughing up a frightened fifteen-year-old who had just come in from the city.

Dale wasn't even roughing me up on purpose. He'd just slap the side of my face or grab a clump of my hair and shake me around like a Rottweiler would shake a rag doll because that was his way. Dale figured he had a mission. He was looking after me for the summer while my parents were away on business and by the autumn I was going to be elevated from the weaknesses he believed all urban children suffered from: cowardice, lack of conviction, and a predilection towards stuttering.

"You're too soft," he would say and shake his head. "People will take advantage of that. They can smell weakness a mile away."

He drove his red Ford on the wrong side of the yellow line, threw beer tins out the window and turned the radio up to full volume while we were stopped at intersections. CKDA, The Voice of The Prairies In Stereo annoyed everyone within a six-car radius. He instructed me to keep my eyes peeled for "the bulls" and stared down other town folk in sedans or coupes who cast him disapproving looks.

"I've got a surprise for you," he said as he spun his Ford across the Red Deer River bridge. Hoodoos, dried cottonwood, and trailer parks all flew past the window far too quickly and another surprise didn't sound like such a good idea. I'd already had enough for one summer: a fist fight at a union hall meeting, dandelion wine that had infected my bladder, and a hay-stacking lesson that lasted well on past midnight. Dale and his wife, Arlene, entertained the neighbours in a homemade sauna and made noises I did not think it was possible for human beings to make. They listened to Charlie Parker nightly on their console at distorted volume and gave me long lectures about the sex lives of extinct Cretaceous animals, which made Dale laugh and Arlene run her tongue over the top of her nicotine-stained teeth. Of course I could have phoned my parents at any time and asked to be sent to my grandmother's house, but we all knew that would mean a lifetime defeat lasting into eternity and so I endured.

"A real friggin sweet surprise," Dale said. He chewed on a toothpick and that dreadful smile crept along his mouth that meant I was in deep trouble. "Aren't you curious? Don't you need to know?"

"I guess," I said.

"Atta boy. Tell you what. The two of us are going to drive up to the old oil rig, have a few brew, and bang off a couple of rounds on my Colt 45. That's a revolver. Ever shot a revolver?"

"No."

Dale laughed. For some reason this was stupendously amusing. "No, I didn't think so. Ever seen a gun? Even know what a gun is?"

Enfields, Stens, Lugers. I knew. "My dad was in the war," I said.

Dale squeezed the toothpick between his lips but he didn't find my part of the story funny at all. "Yeah, well you weren't. I can't say for your dad. I guess he had enough over there in the big WW Two. But I will tell you this: we got to get you young fellas trained up tough before this goddamn Lester Pearson turns us all into a bunch of peace-loving flakes. I bet you vote Liberal don't you?"

"I'm fifteen."

"Yeah, of course." Dale let whatever line of rhetoric he was pursuing fall away. That was one of the great things about Dale. He'd get all serious for a minute then forget what he was talking about the next. He ran his thumb under the strap of his dirty brown coveralls and formulated the rest of his egregious plan. "I'll make an even sweeter deal with you. We'll go up to the rocking horse plant. It's my most favourite spot on earth. If we pull this off, I mean if you can hit anything, we'll have a party. Get some weed and some Jack Daniel's, maybe even have a few girls over. You like girls, don't you? Please tell me you do. I know a few who just love the young ones."

"What would Arlene say?"

Dale rolled his eyes. His fingers curled around the steering wheel and he stared at some far away point amongst the bitter bush. "Oh, Jesus," was all he muttered.

The rocking horse station was pretty much like you would think. A rusted blue petroleum plumber that had ceased working when the price of oil fell off; it cowered at the end of a dusty road forsaken and sad. Surrounded by tin huts and cacti, you knew this was the place people came to do what they weren't supposed to, and if they did, they wouldn't get caught. There were a lot of broken bottles and cigarette packs. Dale shut the car off and in a moment the inside of the cab became hot and still. After a few seconds the cicadas started up and I wondered why we weren't getting out. Then he reached behind the seat and pulled out two Black Labels. Beads of ice water ran down the brown glass. How Dale kept beer cold in the middle of summer was a mystery to everyone. We sat in the front seat and drank. The backside of my nose stung of malt. Dale stared out across the obdurate sandstone at a line of pines and didn't say a word, but his lips moved around a string of awkward consonants. The smell of thistle rose up through the floorboards.

"You got to love it here," he said finally.

"Why?" I said.

"Can't you feel it?"

"Feel what?"

"In the air, in the heat, in the trees. The pine trees especially." He gazed at me and I saw how grey his eyes were and how rumpled his face had suddenly become. He was, I suppose, a desperate man always, but then it really showed. There was something he was begging me to pick up on, but being fifteen and too green, I was not able. "Never mind. Come on. Let's poke a few weasels."

Dale had the revolver in his left hand. The ugly chunk of metal sucked up the sunlight and just about anything else that came close.

"Did you have that in your coveralls?" I said.

"Of course I had it in my coveralls. A man needs to have protection on his person. What good is it going to do me at home or locked up in a box? This isn't goddamn Vancouver and I ain't no rich engineer."

Dale clearly had a predilection against cities, where I was from, and engineers, which my father was one of, and rich, which he wasn't. He rolled the cylinders over in the gun and the tumblers made a clicking noise. His mouth formed an O as they clicked, like he really enjoyed the act and so I figured it was time to get out of the truck.

I set up a row of soup tins on the ledge of the rocking horse. The metal was hot in the sun and the No Trespassing sign had been riddled with buckshot. I was pretty sure Dale wouldn't start shooting while I was setting up the tins. Not on purpose, anyway, but I had lost count of the number of times he had done something stupid when I had told myself he wouldn't: cleaned the toilet plug with sulfuric acid, propositioned the on-duty constable for a quickie, or fixed the clothesline with a chainsaw. It never worked. Then when it was all over, he would just shrug, say sorry, and walk away.

When I got back to the firing line, Dale slapped the revolver down in my palm. "Rule one," he said. "Don't be afraid of your weapon. Don't ever be afraid of a friggin gun."

"I'm not afraid of it."

"Yeah, yeah, sure. Listen, either you are in control or the gun is. Just like with a horse. Or a woman. Take command." Dale got behind me in sort of a rear nelson bear hug. His arms were around my elbows, his chin was on my shoulder. His breath smelled of beer and his bristles cut into my cheek. "Grab hold with both hands. Not like in the movies. No one-handed shooting out here. That is for gangsters and fags. But listen, here is the secret with the two-handed grip; think love-hate. The inside hand holds the handle real loose, like you're feeling a girl's toushie-tui. The outside hand goes around firm like a Viking holds his sword. Love, hate, get it? Then squeeze the trigger real slow. No jerking. No twitching. The gun should surprise you when it goes off."

Dale was breathing slowly and concentrated harder than I did. My finger slid back. The atmosphere exploded. The round bounced off the rocking horse. Then there was nothing but the cicadas again.

"Well," he said. "You hit something. If the planet earth counts."

Dale took the gun from me and shot all five tins off the rocking horse in rapid-fire succession. He mouthed the word *pow* each time he squeezed off a round. Then he twirled the pistola around his index finger and reached into his vest pocket for more bullets. A second beer bottle got pitched into the air and Dale launched off a round at eleven o'clock high. The beer exploded sending a line of foam across the gulley.

"Fabulous," he said. "Now put a stubby on top of your head."

I knew things were going from crazy to insane and I only wanted to be back in Vancouver where I might live to see another autumn. "That would be stupid," I said.

"What's the matter, are you scared?"

"Scared or not. It would still be stupid."

"You're frightened, aren't you?" Dale pocketed the revolver and pushed his finger into my chest. I didn't do anything so he drew his lips tightly together and leaned into me. "Goddammit. Push me back. Don't let anyone do that to you. Don't ever let anyone tell you to do something dumb then poke you. Hit them in the face, dammit." He closed his eyes and pushed his jaw out. His teeth were huge and yellow. "Go on dammit you little frigger. Hit me. There's monsters out there. Waiting to peck your soul out. I'm doing this for your own good. Hit me."

But I didn't hit Dale so he shoved me backwards and I tripped over the beer case and my head struck a rock. I thought I heard a gecko play a blue accordion, but of course there weren't any blue accordions or geckos in our Albertan gulley in the last week of August. There was just blood soaking through my hair and the next thing I knew Dale was kneeling beside me wiping up the mess with his very best handkerchief. This was the one he wore to square dances so he must have felt at least some bad. "Jesus, kid. I am sorry. I was just trying to help out. Look, have some more beer. Not a word to your parents, okay? Let's forget about the hitting stuff. Your dad was right, fighting is bad. I'll tell you what, you throw a couple of bottles in the air and watch me blast them and you'll feel better. I'll give you five bucks if I don't hit one. No, wait, ten."

Dale fumbled to open a brownie. Then he watched me drink the beer and lifted his eyebrows in approval when I downed half the bottle at once. I hadn't much liked the taste of malt two months ago. But every day I was starting to like it more. My scalp had stopped bleeding and the beer was going to my head so I forgave Dale, stood up, and took two Black Labels out of the case. I threw them into the air then ducked like an air raid was imminent. Dale drew up too quickly, fired and the windshield of his truck erupted into a supernova of glass.

There wasn't much either of us could say. Maybe I hadn't picked the best direction to toss the bottles. Probably he shouldn't have pushed me down. Either way, forty years of bad living were catching up with him right at that very moment and there was nothing he could do but puff his cheeks and blow. A magpie mocked us from the far side of the ancient creek bed.

"Well, I guess we'll be walking home," Dale said. "There's enough weed AWOL in that truck to have us locked up forever if we get stopped by the bulls. And with no windshield we'd get stopped for sure. Come on partner. We'd better go and face the music. Arlene is going to have my head on a platter."

He slapped me on the shoulder. Then we both opened another Black and started the long walk home with the case tucked under his arm and the Colt stuffed somewhere down his pants.

"Well, what did you think of the shooting?" he said when we were out on the main highway.

"It was good," I said, although I hadn't really got to do all that much.

"Bet your old man never let you do that."

I didn't really like him calling my father my old man so I just shook my head in agreement. "This is what summers are for," he said. "You're probably way happier here than wherever the hell your parents went this summer. Where the hell did they go and why?"

"Moscow. My father is selling turbines to the Russians."

"Communists," he said.

A yellow Dodge rambled down the road beside us and a blonde woman leaned around the window and waved at Dale. Her hair blew around in the wind as she blew him a kiss.

"Hey, that's Fiona," Dale said and shouted for them to stop. The woman threw a flower out the window, but the car kept on going and the horn made a long dying sound as the silhouette of metal disappeared into the horizon. "Dammit. Those little foxes. Too cheap to stop for the likes of us right now. Maybe we'll get them over tonight. Do you like blondes or brunettes? It's all the same to me. You could like redheads for all I care. Hell, you could be into boys. I was just pulling your tail back there. You can screw whoever you like around here. That's what I love about this valley. You can believe in whatever you want and everything still works out."

But as soon as we got to the driveway, I knew everything wasn't going to work out. The screen door was ajar and a strange voice came from the kitchen. Dale and Arlene's kitchen was right out of a black and white television show: bleak tile floor, plain white table cloth, bare cupboards, and square chrome appliances. Arlene sat in the corner smoking. She was a redhead all right, with a full fury of country dress and always looking slightly annoyed. In a way it made her look both dangerous and sexual. A young man sat at the table with a black suitcase by his knees. He was two years my junior, but tall and doing his best to look older with a ripped jean jacket and a curl of auburn hair oiled to his forehead.

Dale and Arlene stared off at each other for a long time. There were other sounds in the kitchen at that moment. The sprinkler in the background, a bottlenose fly bumping up against the window sill, and a coffee pot perking on the stove, but you could tell some kind of radio waves were passing between their two minds that drowned everything else out.

"Dale, this is Kevin," Arlene said.

Dale had this stupid grin pasted to his face. Like something he'd suspected for a long time had finally caught up to him and there was no place to run.

"Go on outside," Arlene said to Kevin and for some reason I followed. We went out onto the gravel driveway and the door slammed behind us. Kevin spat on one of the round white stones

MARTIN WEST

and pulled out a package of cigarettes. They were the same kind Arlene smoked.

"You're not so smart you know," Kevin said to me.

"Who said I was?"

"Arlene told me that your family is rich and your dad is some kind of brain doctor. Well, it obviously didn't get passed down."

"Who are you, anyhow?"

Kevin lit up a cigarette and blew a column of nicotine into the hot Badland air. The smoke stayed motionless for the longest time before gathering enough initiative to move on. All at once it dawned on me that Kevin had the same pouty mouth that Arlene had. He smoked in the same screw-you way and flicked his head back in a fashion that declared the world owed him a lot.

"Arlene was married before Dale if that helps you," he said.

"Does Dale know?"

From inside the house the tenor of voices rose in a clatter. Finally Arlene shouted and the coffee pot smashed through the window. The glass cascaded down in crystal stalactites and the coffee grounds ran in a trail of brown fluid down the cement steps.

"He does now," Kevin said. He stared at the end of the cigarette like it might facilitate some solution to the dilemma.

"Where is your father?" I said.

"Threw me out," Kevin shrugged. It sounded like this wasn't the first time. "He's not a bad guy though. Tough bitch. Not like Dale here. What a screw-up."

From the inside of the house came a broken whimper of a large bird striking a windshield and I knew Dale was sobbing.

"See what I mean?" Kevin said.

"This is not a good place to be now."

"Where the hell are you going?"

"Down to the river," I said, and didn't ask him to come along.

"The river? Rivers are for fags."

His voice got farther and farther away and soon I was at the edge of Dale's property with the dead caragana leaning over the cliff and cattle wire snarling the sage. I might have been intent on escaping my summer filled with family monsters but one of Kevin's well-aimed rocks struck me on the back of my shoulder. I tumbled down the cliff through the ancient layers of sandstone and ate a cow-pie at the water's edge.

My scalp bled again but this time there were no blue geckoes standing above me, only a winged reptilian figure with red hair and a jean jacket. Kevin barred my way and smacked a sage bough across his hand like a school principal about to administer a beating. Along with my second concussion there was little else I could do but feel like prey and empty my bladder into my jeans.

"Where the hell did you fall to?" he said.

To this day, I am positive I spoke. I am sure I said; "To a place you never will." I'm sure at least the words had formed in my mind and my lips were moving, but also moving were cirrus clouds across a pink sky, raven feathers in the summer breeze and a combine over the rippling field.

"Well, you sure missed the fireworks up there," Kevin said and swatted the sage against his jacket. "Dale and Arlene pretty much replayed the Battle of the Somme."

It wasn't hard to deduce that Kevin made his living by spotting the weakness in other people and there was no doubt a lot of weakness to be spotted in me then. My fingers tingled, the back of my scalp was crusted with blood, and my vision was clouded with animals that did not exist.

"What the hell is the matter with you?" Kevin said. "You look like you have the palsy. Didn't your mother ever to tell you to keep your mouth shut when you were talking to your elders?"

Kevin took a step closer and whiffed the scorching air. "Well, oh my Jesus. What have we got here? Have you gone and wet yourself? Wasn't your mother present to change your diapers?" My mother's cousin's wife's relative then turned around and raised both hands to the heavens. "Arlene you'd better get out here. This is an emergency. Dale's nephew has gone and pissed himself again."

Kevin waited a few seconds, not to see if Arlene would come out, but to make sure that she wasn't and then he closed the single step between us.

"Since Arlene can't come and be your nursemaid," he said, "it looks like I'll have to take care of you."

Kevin gave my chest a jab with his finger. When I didn't move he laughed and slapped the side of my face while cooing a long string of insults that didn't make much sense syntactically. It wasn't that I couldn't move, it was more that my temporal, occipital, and frontal lobes were preoccupied with how a gecko could become such an ugly creature and descend across Dale's river. How could it even get off the ground? Why did everything still smell like urine? Kevin stepped on my foot and then he spat in my face. I calculated the number of flaps per second the creature would have to make to stay airborne at our altitude. Kevin took my palm, rubbed it into my crotch then shoved my fingers in my mouth.

Then I felt greatly saddened that I hadn't been able to hit anything with Dale's revolver. Angered, actually. Enraged. I seized Kevin's collar with one hand and buried my fist into his nose with the other. His cartilage cracked and so I struck it again and again until he crumpled to his knees. I struck him in the cheek and the eyes and the temple, too. Red snot came out of his nose and he flopped over a bed of wild roses and so I kicked him in the chest and stomach and then, for good measure, in the groin. His foot made a twitching motion that reminded me of the song "When The Red-Red Robin Comes Bob-Bob-Bobbing Along." And then I just left him in the dirt and walked around the juniper bush back to the house.

Dale was sitting on the concrete bird bath near the garage smoking a cigarette and staring up into the sky. His face was worn and his eyes were wet and it was not hard to detect that my most favourite relative was very alone in this world. He examined me the same way he had surveyed his gulley-ridden kingdom only a few hours before, then saw Kevin's figure sprawled at the end of the yard. There must have been some sort of proof or at least promise there, because he got up, came over, and gazed into my numb face.

"What did you see at the river?" he said.

He held me close and I felt his rugged hands on my shoulder and those great grey eyes on my brow, begging so badly for something to be taken back or needing so desperately to give it all away.

THE FETISH

DUST DEVILS TWISTED down Railway Avenue all the time in the autumn. Thistles and memories from the Great Depression were a happening that people liked for sentimental reasons. But Edmund did not like them. Not one bit. They left him afraid and torpid in the afternoon sun. He recited prayers for consolation and algebraic theorems for comfort. In the alcove of Dennis Drugs, he waited until the funnel cloud passed over the Cobalt Hotel. Then he locked his bicycle to the rack and went inside. He stumbled through the thirteenth Psalm and put his prescription basket on the counter.

"Did you say something?" Dennis said.

"I didn't say anything."

"You were talking to somebody."

"Not to you."

Dennis handed down the delivery manifest on a clipboard with a sack of medications.

"Can you deliver these?"

"Are there any for Miss Diesbert?" Edmund said.

"Do the lawyers' office first."

"Lawyers are a soiled lot."

Edmund was six feet tall and one hundred and forty-two pounds. He was eighteen years old yet did not possess a driver's licence. When his reflection stopped him at the glass transom, he wiped a stain off the window with his cuff and wished that none of those facts were true.

Dennis stepped off his podium. "Are you are all right?"

"The dust devils give me sinus trouble."

"Are you well enough to deal with my customers is what I'm asking."

"I have always dealt with your customers properly."

Dennis scratched his head because at least that much was true. "Take a pair of sunglasses off the shelf. They'll keep the thistle out of your eyes."

Edmund paused by the stand for a moment then reached out to the vulgar fruit. He picked a gold pair with pink surfboards on the arms. In front of the mirror, he ripped off the price tag, slipped them over his eyes and realized how much he looked like a movie star or a skydiver.

Outside, another twister lit up by Bricker's Hardware. The spiral spun filth, cherry branches, and pin-up girls to the top of a light standard where they collected in a swarm.

Edmund glided out onto Second Avenue and endured the slaughter of shoelaces and sparrows that blistered from the gutter in the same way he recalled fire blistering from the hell bends of church textbooks. When the icy-blue lure of the Sugar Freeze caught his attention, he was calmed by the pale glass and suddenly very thirsty.

Inside, the restaurant's door closed behind him and transformed the room into a soundless space station, silent and separated from the fury of the autumn chaos. There was the smell of ice cream and blueberry sauce. Of cola and peppermint. The counter was chrome and the signs above the kitchen advertised larger than life fruit drinks that glowed orange. Edmund advanced to the register. He asked for a strawberry slushy and put his hands on the curved metal. Its perfection made him feel chaste.

"What size?" the girl said. She wore a white service blouse. Her face was smooth and her lip invited a virtue Edmund thought worth redeeming.

"The largest one possible," he said.

She rang the purchase on the register. "It's warm enough."

"Have you noticed exactly how warm?"

"Global climate change."

"Two and a half degrees centigrade warmer than normal."

"That would account for the whirlwinds," she said.

"You've seen them?"

"They're hard to ignore." She ran her finger down the price list menu.

"Have you noticed they possess so much more intent than before?"

"Not really."

"Like they know exactly where they're going."

"All I know is they put dents in my car."

Edmund leaned over the counter. "It is their impurity."

The young girl hit the sale button on the till and a green light came on. "That will be two-eighty-seven."

"They are unclean."

"Are you Mormon?"

"No."

"It's still two-eighty-seven."

"I can expunge that contaminant."

It was all so simple and he knew it was a mistake right away, but already he had reached out across the counter of misinterpretation and then it was too late. The girl recoiled. There was the sound of a buzzer going off and a manager in a stuffed green shirt appeared from the kitchen with a brass spatula in his hand.

Outside, a convective cell flew across the parking lot. In its clutches spun twig bark, hawk feathers, bobby pins, and a licence plate from Manitoba. The metal scraped the window with a scream so deep Edmund fled through the eastern exit to escape his concupiscence, the store manager, and whomever else might come bent on vengeance.

CHANTAL DIESBERT WAS waiting for him in the window when he rode his bicycle to her driveway. She lived in a small brick bungalow with a large mountain ash in the middle of the lawn. She wore a white blouse, plastic apron, and a curious tight dress that had dropped in from another era to end just above her knees.

Her doorbell was blue porcelain. The buzz echoed through the hallway for a long time. A raven crossed the skyline. When she answered the door, she had applied lipstick to a scar that fish hooked over her jaw.

"You are late," she said.

"Forgive me."

Edmund stepped out of a dry continental climate into astute silence. The inside of Chantal's house was hardwood and immaculately cleaned. The walls were decorated with minimalist landscapes. Two chairs, one white sofa, and an alabaster plant stand in the living room.

"I have your prescription, Miss Diesbert," he said.

"You may call me Miss Chantal now you are inside." She checked once on the porch, closed the door and slid the deadbolt into place. Then she extended her palm towards the kitchen.

All the light inside Chantal's house was cream and thin. The walls had been modified with glass blocks popular during the 1970s. The kitchen was both immense and untouched. Marble counters, Scandinavian chairs, and a wood cooking island in the middle of the void.

Edmund stood behind the table with his hands folded on his belt and the white paper bag floating on the pine. Gravity might be ignored. Chantal receded to a wicker chair and steepled her fingers. Her square and handsome face quivered as she spoke. "Take the medication out of the bag and count the pills," she said.

Edmund took a pair of scissors from a wooden block on the counter and clipped off a corner of the paper bag. Then he removed the bottle, twisted the cap, and carefully rolled the sixty tablets out onto the wood.

"They are all here, Miss."

"Count them out in pairs."

He counted them out in twos, pushing the pills to the centre of the counter so his host could observe their perfection. At pill thirty-three, Edmund paused. His finger deflected the rest of the pink ovals to the eastern periphery of the island. For a few seconds they rattled on the precipice then Edmund corralled them into his palm and plunged the medication into his pocket. Chantal nodded as if listening to a beautiful fugue in the summer air.

"Late afternoon is my most favourite time of day," she said.

"Will there be anything else, Miss Chantal?"

"One thing, Edmund."

"Yes, Miss."

She signed the delivery manifesto that appeared from beneath her arm and nodded. "When you are finished disposing of the paperwork, you must set some traps for me."

"Traps, Miss?"

"For rats. They are running rampant. I don't have a single fitness magazine that is safe."

"We don't have rats in this province," he said.

"They leave chunks of their rotting tails all over my paper plates."

"It is too cold in the winter, Miss Chantal."

"Then they could be bats or scarabs. Pterodactyls for all I care. They scuttle behind the plaster at night and unnerve me greatly."

Edmund dropped the prescription bag into a white trash can then walked over to the wall. He placed his ear to the plaster. The paint had been worn thin and on a thumb tack next to the air vent hung a dried Sani-Wipe.

"I can't hear anything," he said.

"Listen harder."

"It is quiet."

"You know there are vermin and they have to be done away with."

"I know, Miss."

"I want you to get down on your hands and knees and check every single hole, dropping, and scratch mark in this house. Do you understand?"

"Of course."

He got down on his knees to inspect the boards. One-inch

maple. A circular air vent had been drilled into the lower wain-scoting, but the filter paper over the entry was unblemished.

"Don't miss anything," she said.

"I can't see anything."

"Then try the plumbing."

Edmund went to the kitchen and opened the cupboards. The garbage pail was lined with a white sheath and filled with oatmeal protein shots that smelled vacantly of rubbing alcohol. The drainpipes that came down from the sink had been polished until they glimmered.

"It looks clean, Miss," he said.

"Then you'll have to inspect the electrical system." She stood in the corner of the living room with her back against the wall and her arms folded. Her spine was straight and in her tall pumps she appeared as an industrial worker from the 1950s. Every time Edmund opened a wiring panel, she sucked back on her cigarette until her jaw trembled.

On the port side of the foyer sat a second panel, used to monitor the air purifying system on which Chantal had spent thousands. He opened the box up and examined the fuses. Even the microchips used to regulate the ion content in the air were scrubbed.

"Not that either," he said.

"How about the utilities?"

"Utilities?"

"The water meter, the natural gas. All that filthy gas coming into my residence, and none of it is accounted for or even screened. Those creatures could be swimming up the pipes."

"How would do they do that?"

"They'd hold their breath."

Edmund proceeded to the indoor metal gas meter. He opened the hatch and waited. A thin curl of glycol rose from the spigot.

"No," she said. "Do it like you are fixing a puzzle."

"Pardon?"

"Like you are fixing a puzzle. Like there is some kind of conclusion. Like you are labouring over the filthiness of your existence and have come to a resolution."

"I shall try."

"And put on those plastic gloves while you do it. The ones on the table."

The four-legged antique gleamed under a ceiling xenon light. The stone had been rubbed so much that the surface glowed like water. Edmund slipped on the pair of green surgical gloves that were covered with lubricant. Then he got back down on his knees and fumbled over the dials of the meter.

"Make sure everything is secure, Edmund," Chantal said. Her breath became short.

"There is nothing insecure."

"Then it's all safe?" She sucked on her cigarette so deeply her face went purple. Then she abruptly strode across the room and reclined into her pearl sofa.

"It appears very safe."

"Put the screw into the circuit," she said. Her hand fluttered over her apron.

"All right," he said. Edmund found a Phillips screwdriver and twisted the tool into a copper socket. Chantal's thigh muscles tensed into concrete and then her elbow struck the brass pot on the calcite stand. The yellow chrysanthemums crashed onto the floor and shattered into a thousand fragments. Chantal slid onto her knees and for a moment her teeth so white, pearl, and perfect parted in a single gasp. For a few seconds there was complete silence and then the sound of deep exhaling.

At last Edmund's host arose, pushed down the pleat in her skirt, and vanished through the cream light in the hallway towards the bathroom. She tossed her body apron and high heels into a plastic bag that was waiting on the door knob, sealed the ends with a twist-tie, and shoved the heap down the garbage chute. Then she started the shower. Soon, curls of white steam folded out of the bathroom and the entire house smelled of carbolic soap. Edmund sat patiently on the stool beside the foyer staring at the screwdriver in his hand. Chantal stayed in the shower for over twenty minutes and mist clung to the windows of the house. A cactus on the oak coffee table developed a bead of condensation on one of its spines.

When she got out of the shower she donned a white jump-suit that an airline stewardess might have worn then went to the kitchen sink and brushed her teeth. She used three different kinds of paste and flossed succinctly while humming "Amazing Grace" into the fogged kitchen window. After, she wiped down all of her fingers with a surgical towelette and returned to her sitting chair. She leaned back and gazed vacantly up through her sunroof to a poplar tree that hovered outside.

"I don't date," she said.

"I'm sorry, Miss?"

"Never mind."

Chantal led Edmund to the door. The moment he was outside the whirl of a vacuum cleaner echoed off a cattle fence and on the horizon a chorus of dust rose up towards the sun.

CRETACEA

A WHITETAIL DEER went down over a wire fence and lay sprawled in the middle of the road right on the centre line. The animal contorted on the pavement with a broken leg in the shadow of the old red wheat king and so I put a single .3o3 round through its head. Part of the skull blew off into the ditch and one of its antlers spun across the pavement to the shoulder. It was the only humane thing to do. Problem was, I wasn't finished shooting stuff then. I lined up a couple of abandoned televisions that a pawnshop had dumped down by the petrified oyster bed and blew the screens out. They imploded with a sucking sound and one of the 1950s style knobs shot into the sky like fireworks. After that, I walked down the street and shot out a few lamp standards and three car windows: a Dodge, a Ford, and a Toyota 4x4, I think. On the edge of town, I perched myself on a big drumlin so I could get a good view of Main Street. Everything was mine for the taking. I took a store window with a garden gnome on display and a fourteen-foot plastic Triceratops that floated above one of the department stores. The beast was filled with helium and attached by a long string to a fire hydrant. The green shimmering body bobbed slowly in the evening breeze, so basically it was an easy target.

Next, I blew apart the golden clown that was embossed on a mock chapel of a hamburger restaurant and put a round into the gut of a dead cat that had been lying for three days on the corner of Main and Second Avenue. Nobody had bothered to pick it up. As for the ecumenical brass clown, that thing had always bothered me a lot, and I felt much better after filling his orange hair with lead.

In a few minutes, the sound of police cars and fire engines filled the streets of our little prairie town, so it was probably time to start the long walk back home. Besides that, I was almost out of ammunition. Half an hour later when I arrived back at my bungalow in the middle of a sage field at the bottom of the Red Deer valley not much had changed. My satellite dish in the willows had still not been hooked up, a stack of magazines and books still lay unsorted on the balcony and on the other side of the field in the grey layers of ancient sediment, a thousand prehistoric beasts still slept silent with their secrets.

I went out into the field and put my rifle in a metal tube, dug a small trench at least two feet deep, and buried the weapon as per the instruction in *Soldier of Fortune* magazine. Then I used a rake and piled some rabbit grass over the hole to make sure everything looked natural. Off in the distance the red and blue blinking bulbs of emergency vehicles still flashed away in the twilight like there was a wedding or Christmas celebration going on, but after an hour or so, the lights grew distant and then disappeared altogether. I guess the authorities must have caught someone who they believed was the right person or else just given up.

There was a documentary on channel 273 that looked interesting, called *Last Dreams of the Dinosaurs* but as the dish was still not connected, there was no point in even turning the TV on. Instead, I sat on the back porch with a glass of Canadian Club and read some poetry by Yeats. From time to time, I wished I had someone there to read it with me. I watched the dead sage roll across the road in the purple dusk and dozed off.

EVERY ACTION HAS a reaction, and the smart ones have none, so sure as shoot first thing the next morning a police cruiser came rolling up my driveway. There's a plastic dog that sits at the foot of the driveway with a solar panel on his head and a motion detector embedded in his nose, so every time something passes by, the dog barks and his eyes light up bright red, like he's possessed, but of course, this didn't scare the police away. I was actually out back washing my hands off with vinegar and baking soda, because this dissolves the cordite on palms in case one is subject to scientific tests. I put all of my things down and went inside to put tea or coffee on as this usually makes the police want to stay and chat for a while and many times they have interesting stories to tell. A few years ago, an elderly corporal named Macnee came investigating some cattle thefts, actual cattle rustling, and stayed for over an hour. Macnee wasn't much into poetry, but he became obsessed with my fossil collection and we spent many weekends scouring the Badlands and drinking Black Label beer looking for some kind of missing link. Black Label was his favourite. He didn't drink anything but Black Label. Sometimes fifteen or sixteen in a row. We never found the missing link or any fossils of much significance, but we had a good time drinking on my porch and Macnee suggested I get a dog to keep me company. Sadly, he got transferred to Nova Scotia, because he had embarrassed himself during a drunken rage at the Bronto Inn and I never saw him again.

THE POLICE CAR stopped outside. I dried my hands and opened the screen door and wasn't really prepared for what stood in front of me. An Amazon blonde constable with wisps of yellow hair falling over her forehead and a few dozen freckles spattered on her cheeks leaned against my door frame and chewed on her pencil eraser. I put her at five-nine and the type who spent most of her time finding just the right perfume when she wasn't working out in the gym. She looked me over once and the right-hand corner of her mouth curled up just a little.

"Hello," she said.

"Hello," I said back.

"Want to know why I'm here?"

"Sure," I said. Any reason would be good enough.

"I'm conducting neighbourhood inquiries about the shooting last night," she said and pulled out her notebook. She tried to find an address by the door; there wasn't one.

"Shooting?" I said.

She shrugged and pushed a wad of chewing gum between her front teeth. "Someone went crazy with a gun and shot the town up. Probably drunk or right-wing. Did you see anything?"

I put one hand on the door frame and leaned forward into the crux of my elbow ostensibly to show some sign of naivety, but in effect to get a closer whiff of her perfume. What is that stuff that smells like dust? Patchouli? Petunia? Permian extinction?

"Constable Holocene," I read off her name tag. "I feel like an idiot now. I did hear something last night that sounded like shots. I knew I should have called you."

"Really? About what time?"

"About seven."

"Seven? Are you sure it was that early?"

"Well, I thought so. Wasn't paying that much attention, really. Sometimes the ranchers shoot at cattle pretty close to here, or anything else that moves."

"Yeah," she said. "And they're not supposed to inside city limits. How many shots did you hear?"

"Only two or three."

"That's it? Two or three?"

"Was there more?"

"Maybe," she said. "What direction did they come from?"

"Down the Dinosaur Trail." I pointed way to the west of where the Whitetail had met its merciful demise. "And then they just got fainter towards town."

"Yep," she said, and scribbled a few lines in her notebook. "That'd be it."

"I feel really bad about not reporting last night. It just didn't seem like anything out of the too ordinary."

"This time it was. For this part of the world, anyway."

Then she looked at me with those blue summer eyes and said, "Do you keep any firearms in the house?"

"Not even a BB gun."

"Mind if I have a look?"

"No, of course not, please come in," I said, because, it was a perfunctory question, and I am an expert at spotting those. I ask them so often.

I stepped back. The good constable made a quick reconnoiter of my cluttered living room. She seemed more interested in the stacks of books and catalogued fossils lying around the floor than any location that might conceal a weapon.

"You're into fossils?"

"I'm especially interested in the Juliana deposits."

"And…" she picked up a book off a stack waist high. "Poetry?"

"I do reviews. For a living. Sort of."

"For a magazine?"

"Yes. For a national magazine."

"For that slightly right of centre national magazine or that slightly… "

"Yes, that one."

"Good on you," she said.

"Would you like to have a cup of coffee or tea? I actually have both just about on the brew."

She looked me over again, put the book down and smiled. "I'd really love too. But we have to have a meeting with the Staff Sergeant at nine about the 'incident'." She raised her finger in the air to quote the word.

"Though the leaves are many, the root is one."

"I swayed my leaves and flowers in the sun," she quoted back.

That was really all it took.

IF YOU BELIEVE in God, you will do the following things: 1) Attend all public meetings in the local town hall about shootings or acts of national subversion that have occurred recently in your area; 2) Accept the fact that everyone in your hometown either has a gun or wants a gun or wishes they wanted a gun or wants to do something important with a gun, but if you actually do something with a gun, then this is blasphemous; 3) Try not to throw up when everyone at the meeting is really upset about something that has happened and assumes that their elected leaders are doing nothing because they elected them.

I pass on all three. One far-right-wing group who named

themselves the "White Cattleman's Petroleum Revenge League"
had threatened to ask American President George Bush to send
in the US Marine Corps if local officials weren't going to act
quickly. There was no mention of the Whitetail deer that had
died so pathetically tripping over a wire fence. I figured it might
be fun to watch, (the meeting, not the invasion) and besides,
somewhere in the middle of the night it had occurred to me that
the first round to be dispatched lay somewhere embedded in a
Cervidae carcass not too far from my own home and that had to
be retrieved. Evidence is evidence as they say, and this had to be
dealt with.

I walked down the Badlands road with the smell of sage and
the sound of cicadas in the air. The height of summer shimmered wet off the hot concrete and I knew this was the only place
in the world to be. When I got to the spot where the deer had
died, there was not a hide in sight. No bones. No hooves. No tail.
This was the right place all right, centre of the road right, third
fence post from the creek, directly under the red wheat king that
school kids had painted a giant yin and yang sign on. If one
looked harder at the cracked wood, they would find older scraw-
ling that dated back to the fifties and even one curious faded etch
mark that read, "D-Day Is Ours." But no deer in sight. For a
moment it seemed possible that the police had impounded the
animal for analysis, for lead content, or maybe they would con-
duct a polygraph, but a closer inspection revealed the obvious
truth. In the right-hand lane a thin stain of blood spread out
funnel-like on the road. Bits of squished deer fur had been
ground into pavement and the antler that had scuttled away from
the impact scene lay in the ditch. The Whitetail had been run
over dozens, maybe hundreds of times and reduced to a fuzzy red

smear towards the horizon. In a day or two there would be not a trace left. The chunk of lead would be an indistinguishable metallic shape and the cartridge just another shiny object sinking into the Cretaceous dust of the Badlands.

With some sense of relief, I ventured into the Maple Leaf grocery store to buy beef jerky and a copy of *Prehistoric History Today* before the meeting. The tale of the shooting was on everyone's lips and everybody had a theory. Over nine hundred rounds had been discharged. One round penetrated a sensitive geo-seismic centre and the oil industry in Alberta would surely be ruined for it. Another round was specifically sent through the theological centre of town in order to demoralize the city's righteous population. The actions were terrorist related, but not politically motivated and attributable to a non-sectarian cult group. When I was paying for the beef jerky curiosity got the better of me and so I had to ask,

"So what happened, anyway?"

"You haven't heard?" the clerk said. "Someone shot up the entire town last night."

"The whole town?"

"All of it. There's a lot of bullets lying in bad places."

"Is there a good place for a bullet to be?"

"Maybe in that magazine."

"You don't like it?"

"No, but we sell a lot of copies. I don't get it."

"There's a lot of pictures. Photos. Of stuff that's relevant."

"I don't know why they put it right up front at the check stand, it doesn't belong there."

I stuck a wad of jerky in my mouth and walked to Main Street. I really shouldn't be eating this stuff. It pulls out my fillings and gets stuck between my teeth and then I'm in a bad mood until I can floss it out. Usually I carry emergency floss with me, but the cherry-mint flavour that I buy at Loo's Import Market that comes only from Beijing had not yet arrived this week, so when I went around the corner onto the scene, I was feeling vulnerable and agitated. The place was still a carnage. None of the damage had been repaired. Instead, every site, hole, and perturbation had been cordoned off with yards of yellow police tape and men in suits were doing triangulation with laser theodolites. A few constables leaned against lampposts making sure no one crossed the line. The saddest sight of all was the poor green plastic Triceratops that lay deflated in the middle of the sidewalk with the collar and string still tied around his flat neck. The bullet had pierced his heart and carried on in an unknown direction.

The meeting was housed in the elementary school gymnasium with red and blue lines painted on the floor and the place was packed. They had set out over a hundred metal folding chairs and they were all full, so the next hundred people stood against the walls. A few of them were drinking beer, but no one paid too much attention to that. Lined up against the far wall stood six overweight men in black jeans and black t-shirts. The shirts all had a giant red C printed on the chest with a white skull and crossbones in the centre. They looked very stern and threatening except for their stomachs that folded in two rolls over their belts. They were holding hoods, scrunching them angrily between their fists, which I presume was because the police told them they couldn't wear hoods during public meetings.

Mary Holocene was on duty again and leaned against the back wall under the basketball hoop wall with an elderly sergeant who looked nervous, like maybe he had to offer an explanation for all of this. A wisp of hair fell over her forehead. She seemed pained to be there, too. Every time one of the cattlemen tried to slide a hood over his head, or even got it above crotch level, she raised one finger and shook it until he retreated.

Some things reveal themselves quickly about people who you find attractive or interesting and already I had deduced many things about Mary Holocene. She was a non-career officer by choice and no doubt came to the force through some biographic accident. By looking at her, I could also tell she probably had some dark or at least embarrassing secret in her past that she wanted to forget or bury so deep that not even the earth would know. The most fun about revealing truths about people who you are attracted to or interested in, is deducing what their deep and dark secrets are and where they lay. Burying the secrets deeply would be an essential component for Mary to leave her past behind and embark on a life change in a paramilitary organization. She would have to convince the polygraph examiner that either the perturbations didn't exist or else that there was really nothing wrong with them. But what could those acts be? This was the stuff that novels are made of. No doubt, Mary as a small girl stole pears, hot-knifed hash oil and attended "Love-Ins" at Stanley Park (she was brought up on the West Coast), or doused her Barbie with kerosene and set it ablaze until it spread to the curtains or carport or perhaps a slumbering cat. But then, every Canadian child does these kinds of things and this is nothing to be ashamed of. No, I could sense Mary's perversions ran deeper than this. No doubt they were formulated during her adolescent or pubescent years. Perhaps they involved strange interactions with older men or retired schoolmarms. Candle wax or Catholic school clothing may have been utilized. But even this was not the elixir. The event would come years later. Some archeological ego-versus-id metaphor that her partner could not understand. Frustrated, she left the relationship and then left town, trying to leave the remnants behind in the gathering dust. But this is not an easy thing to do. Mary soon found that she was only attracted to others with a perverse mindset such as her own and constantly had to be leaving affairs and leaving towns for lack of satisfaction and growing security concerns. Then one day in desperation, when towns had run out, she visited a recruiting office and a few weeks later found herself at the training depot in Regina. These things happen.

The inside of the gymnasium was getting very hot and droplets of clear sweat had spattered on the shiny floor. I wandered down to a pop machine and dropped a loonie in the slot. The coin rattled into the guts of the machine, but nothing came out, so I dropped another inside and the same thing happened. I had a pocketful of change, so I went over to the next machine and tried a third time. Three bucks gone now, never to be returned. There's no point in shaking or kicking these machines so I moved down to the fourth dispenser in the line and gave it one last shot. This time a soda rolled out at the bottom and then two more followed it. I had an idea.

With three tins in hand, I walked back to the gymnasium. Under the basketball hoops, still leaning against the wall were Mary and her sergeant. I offered them both unopened tins.

"Thanks," the sergeant said. "I've got to get up in front of these morons in a minute and tell them everything that I don't know. My throat is bone dry." He took the tin and swallowed half of it in one gulp.

"You looked like you were having problems with the machines there," Mary said.

"Yeah, you have more patience than I do," the Sergeant added. "I would have shot the damn thing."

The three of us grunted a laugh, but not too loud, because shooting wasn't that funny a topic on this occasion.

Mary told the sergeant that I did poetry reviews for national magazines.

"Really?" the sergeant said. He was thinking about his upcoming speech and had the jitters. He played with his tie clip. "Which ones?"

I ambled off a rather long and detailed list.

"Good for you," he said. "I like books. Especially books about fishing."

Mary nodded and understood the names didn't mean much to the sergeant. What I said was actually true. I have published reviews in such magazines, but I wasn't going to volunteer the information that my last three publications had been in *Screw, Hustler,* and *The Northern Beaver.*

The meeting got going. I spent most of my time sneaking peeks at Mary's vest-covered breasts and trying to smell her cologne.

THE INVESTIGATORS OF the incident had determined a number of facts. First, that all of the targets were hit at long range. Second, the weapon used was probably a .303 with old ammunition. Perhaps even war ammunition that had been stored in a cold dry place. Third, every target had only one bullet in it and no "stray" shots have yet to be found, meaning that either the shooter was an expert marksman or had a scope with remarkable precision. Fourth, that the targets all seemed to be of a symbolic nature and the Sergeant appeared pleased with the use of this word, like he had just picked it up in something other than a police manual. Last, that sadly as of yet there were no suspects—although some interesting leads had been uncovered, there was simply nowhere to go. This bought an angry cry from the black-shirted Cattleman's Revenge League who hooted and hollered that the police were in cahoots with eastern Liberals and that if everyone could carry a gun around with them then the shootist would have been shot dead before he did any more property damage and land owning people should be entitled to shoot things out as they so wished. Generally, the crowd didn't side with the cattlemen, and the sergeant, no greenhorn at dealing with angry people, concluded by adding that this incident could have been the work of extremists, which shut the cattlemen up right quick and made at least half the crowd cast disapproving glances back at the four fat men who now looked rather silly holding black hoods somewhere around crotch level.

Even a small town has its dark side when it comes to humour and our little town is no exception. The community cable channel has a weekly comedy spot that is actually filmed in a store front window of a women's dress shop off Main Street. People stop and watch it being filmed with bundles of hockey sticks or tubs of antifreeze under their arms, not because they think the show is wise or funny, but because they want to catch a glimpse of themselves on television the following Wednesday when the show is aired.

This week they had three contestants who insisted that they were the "shootist" and were trying to prove it to the game host by answering tricky historical questions. The contestants were Karl Marx, Indira Gandhi, and Ivan the Terrible. Jesus Christ had been pulled at the last minute and so one chair was vacant. One of the producers had said to his director that this was still a Christian town and Jesus Christ had better not show up on the set if they wanted any funding next year. As I sat inside the store watching the show, it occurred to me that all of these people wanted to be the shootist. The Cattleman's Petroleum League wanted to be the shootist. The grocery store clerk wanted to be the shootist. When Ivan the Terrible was asked at the end why he thought the audience should vote for him as the shootist, he replied, "Because then at last everybody would know who I am."

Outside the mall cum TV studio, I asked a construction worker, a gas station attendant, a bus driver, and a very modern nun who wore a blue suit with a red tie who they thought Ivan the Terrible was, and none of them knew.

On my way home, I walked by the animal shelter and thought I'd better ask one more person to make the study scientific. Inside, a pimply high school student leaned over an aluminum counter reading a super hero comic book. There was a bucket filled with disinfectant and a mop behind him, but he didn't appear too interested in scrubbing the floor. When I asked him who Ivan the Terrible was he said, "Didn't he have something to do with the shooting?"

"Shooting?"

"Yeah, shooting. Don't you know? Do you want a dog?" he asked.

"Not really, why?"

"Because this is the pound."

"No thanks," I said.

"Then why did you come in here? Don't you have a job?"

"Yes, I have a job," I said. "I work in the publishing industry, actually. Aren't you going to clean that floor?"

He looked down at the bucket and then back at me. "No. Take a dog, would you, mister."

"Don't want one."

"Then we have some old dogs that won't live very long. You'd only have to put up with it for a little while before it died so it wouldn't be much of an investment."

"I'm not sure if that's a good deal or not. What would I do with a dog anyway?"

"It'd keep you company when you're lonely," he said.

I thought about it for a moment. "What kinds of dogs do you have?"

"All kinds. Big ones. Black ones. Small ones."

"What would you recommend?"

"Well, personally I'd take one that's been here the longest so it doesn't get put down. That's sometimes very traumatic for them."

"Okay, show me."

The young boy put a tick in the right-hand column of the white folder he had on the counter and took me to the back of the pound that smelled like dog fur and disinfectant. In the last cage, an ugly black dog cowered in the rear of the run. Long whiskers stuck out of his snout and white froth bubbled around his mouth. He looked like some combination of Heeler and Lab.

"I'll throw in a leash for free if you take him," the boy said.

"Free leash?"

"No charge. A collar, too."

"All right," I said.

The boy did the paperwork then got the black dog from the cage and found a leash and collar. The dog sat there patiently in the front office wondering what kind of unhappiness he'd got himself into this time, but figuring it was better than whatever awaited him in the cage. I clicked the leash onto his collar and we walked out the front door together. For the first few blocks the dog was enthusiastic to be outside, he looked from side to side, sniffed at rabbit grass and growled at a mailbox like he was looking after me, but after a while he slowed to a geriatric crawl and finally by the bridge that crossed the Red Deer River under the giant green T. rex, the dog sat down on the hot sidewalk and would go no further. I picked the animal up, but it was too heavy to carry more than a few steps so outside the Dixie Queen with yellow Durham husks in the air, we stood with no resolution.

A police car stopped at the corner and Mary rolled down her electric window.

"New dog?" she said.

"Well, he's new to me. I just got him and he's too old to make the trip home."

Mary bit her lip, adjusted her rearview mirror then popped the electric lock on the passenger side. "Get in," she said.

I sat in the front seat with the dog on my lap. The inside of the car smelled like IsoGel. Mary started down the country road. She talked as she drove and steered the car with one hand. We bounced over a set off railway ties at 105 kilometres an hour.

"Isn't this against policy?" I asked.

"Probably," she said and drove on with her right hand on the emergency brake. "What made you decide to get a dog?"

"I'm not sure. He was in the cage by himself and looked lonely. Besides, the guy in the pound assured me that he was a good copy editor."

She laughed and was going to say something but then the dispatcher on the radio called her in a scratchy voice that only police can understand. Apparently, a tractor had overturned on the high-way and some pigs were pinned under the rear wheels.

"Oh ferfuksakes," Mary muttered and pushed the car up to a hundred and thirty. She slid sideways in a cloud of dust near my driveway and popped up the door locks.

"Got to run," she said.

I got out and walked the dog back to the house. Inside, I found a big wicker basket that had been used to store magazine reviews and put some blankets inside. The dog curled up and went to sleep. Later that evening, I made hamburgers and the dog ate a whole paddy and we sat out on the porch drinking rye watching the summer sun turn red into twilight.

THE TOP HALF of the ridge caught fire the next afternoon while the dog and I were down on the back porch dozing. The dog was in his basket curled up like a doughnut and only shifted from side to side as the first particles of soot settled on the unpainted cedar strips around him. One moment the edge of the coulee was brown and still the next minute it was jumping with bright yellow flames. Thousands of sparks flew into the air as the rabbit grass ignited and then the sky filled with sweet grey smoke as the sage began to burn. It was all very exciting. Reams of smoke rolled down the coulee like waves breaking on a beach and the smell of autumn filled the valley bottom. Cacti make strange popping sounds when they burn under very high temperatures and all of the eastern slopes were now bursting like tiny landmines. To add to the excitement, I lit up a Camel cigarette that a friend of a friend had assured me was in the back pack of an actual GI at Quê So'n during the Vietnam War. The dog rolled over and chewed on a biscuit and I decided since it was after four o'clock, (one minute after, actually) having the first rye of the day would be okay. I have rye with all kinds of things: with ginger ale, and root beer, with tomato juice, and lemon water. Sometimes, I have rye with ice and sentimental objects in the bottom of the glass for flavour. A spike taken from the Canadian Pacific Railway. A piece of chopstick from Mrs. Chung's Chinese Restaurant on Fourth Avenue who serves amazing almond chicken. A shred of the original Canadian Constitution Act that was torn from the Senate Chambers when Pierre Elliot Trudeau signed it in 1980, or so my source tells me. About the only thing I can't drink rye with is milk, and that's probably got something more to do with the aesthetics of the milk curdling like the satellite photo of the moon than with the actual taste. Today I had it straight though, no mixing necessary, because the reality of something exciting happening on your own back door adds its own flavour to the rye.

Just to keep things safe, I went down into the basement and got a hundred feet of irrigation tubing that the previous owner had left behind when he'd sold the house. I hooked the hose to the faucet under the bathroom window. The faucet was huge and probably used for farm purposes because a lot of pressure came out the end. I drenched the roof and walls of the house and then dragged the hose as far out back as it would go. The hose and me ended up by a windmill with a rooster on top right near a creek that ran through the back of my property. When I opened the spigot, the water squirted another hundred feet towards the coulee. I watered down the single cottonwood in the back field and then sprayed the grass that looked sad and droopy in the August sun. It's pretty hard to tell where my property ends and the grazing lands begin. I have ten acres altogether and the cattle fence that was once at the back of the property has long since fallen down. The ranchers never bothered to put it back up again. I'm not sure if that's because the land down here is no good for cattle or whether the ranchers couldn't care less if the cows wandered onto my property. Anyway, it's all flat down here for a thousand feet until the edge of the Badlands rise up steeply towards the prairie. When the sage on the flats started to burn, the smell was bitter and the bitterness made me think I was in a tomb and, of course, for many ancient animals it was. I started to think about the seasons changing and layers of time being exposed and yielding up their dead and the next thing you know there's half a dozen fire trucks rushing towards me over the grass with their lights red and green spinning away.

I'm not sure how they got so close without me noticing, but the firemen in their heavy burlap coveralls were very excited and shouted instructions at me as if in semaphore. In a way, I was sorry that they showed up. The burning sage was a perfume that made me think of Mary, and how strangely time passed in eons when you were thinking of another person. Then, the grass flames were like fireworks, only better because they raced round in circles and leaped from bush to bush, which is something fireworks can't do.

The fire trucks came to a stop where the playa met the steep cliffs of the Badlands and sprayed everything in sight. They used three hoses held by nine men and they sprayed a dozen bushes at a time with water and white bubbly foam. The foam degraded into a grey sludge that was going to leave a horrible mess all over the bunch grass. One of the firemen even uncoiled a long hose with a filter on the end and ran down to the creek to suck some extra water out. I thought this was uncalled for, because it wasn't really a big fire and I probably could have handled it all myself, if the thing hadn't burnt out on its own accord first.

Then the police showed up. Mary and the sergeant drove right up to my back door and Mary jumped out shouting. I waved to her, but she didn't as much wave back as she motioned frantically for me to come over. At that precise moment a curl of dried grass caught fire just to the east of the tamarack tree and two rabbits squirmed between the two fingers of flames. They ran around and around in circles not going anywhere, so I shut the hose off and walked out through the smoke. The ground must have been hot because even with my rubber boots on the heat came through to my feet and the stench of burnt rubber made me choke. The rabbits were either paralyzed with fear or stunned by the smoke. They just cowered there motionless and I yarded them both up by the scruff of the neck and carried them back to the house. I knew the dog wouldn't chase them because he was still eating biscuits, so I put the rabbits into his basket and covered them up with a red terry cloth.

The fire trucks had driven through the back field and drenched everything that moved. They squirted the "hot spots" a second time after one of the firemen inspected the ground with infrared glasses and then the "big tank" truck drove right up to my house and gave it a precautionary dousing. Problem was, the hose was so strong that it ripped off a dozen shingles and shattered my bathroom window. After they figured they had done enough damage, they gave me a friendly wave and turned the hoses off. The show was over. The fire was out. That's the thing with grass fires. They come and go in an instant and they look worse than they really are.

Mary and the sergeant stood on my back porch. The sergeant had picked up one of the rabbits and held it in his arms. Mary was scratching its neck.

"Do you mind if I keep them?" the Sergeant asked.

"Sure," I said. I had no idea if he wanted them for his kids or if he was going to cook them up in a stew. They weren't really mine to give away.

"Thanks," he said. He picked the second one up and coddled them like he had a newborn set of twins. The four red eyes of the rabbits disappeared into the chest of his khaki uniform. "I'm out of here, Mary. If you want to take care of the report, fantastic. No further action, I think. Glad your house didn't burn down, mister."

"Me too," I said.

The sergeant left with the rabbits. Mary and I stood on the porch looking over the flat valley bottom. The flat earth had a dusting of black soot. A stench of burned bush moved in from the south. On the western horizon, a grey thunderhead rose thousands of feet into the summer sky.

"Good work with the rabbits," she said. "The sergeant loves rabbits."

"I wish they hadn't put all that foam on the ground. It's going to stink. It looks really ugly and it's going to irritate my asthma."

"Better than a burned down house."

"It probably wouldn't have come this far. Besides, grass fires, flash in the pan, so to speak."

"Still, it's a good thing you called."

"I didn't call."

"You didn't?"

"I don't have a phone. There's no phone line in here. The phone company wanted a thousand dollars to hook it up. Got something to do with my distance from the road."

"Don't you have a cellphone?"

"Why?"

"So people who want to get in touch with you, like, say for example, they want to meet with you sometime in their busy schedule, but can't do it because you're not near a landline, they can get you on your cellphone."

Land line? Cellphone? Did I? Yes, I did. The producer of a pornographic film company had once given me a "CellPhone Package Certificate" while drunk one night in a bar after I had done a favourable review of one of his pieces. He must have been desperate.

"The battery is dead," I said. Like I would know. I have never received a call on the phone, never received any billing for it, and have never phoned out.

The dog ambled out into the back field. He was angular as he walked, like maybe his arthritis was giving him problems.

"Let's see it," Mary said.

The cellphone was under a pile of papers beside my desk which sat by the west facing picture window in the living room. Who puts a desk in their living room?

"This is ancient," she said and rolled the bulbous chrome body over her palm.

"I'm not one for technology."

"How about the modern novel?" Mary pried out the spine of the cellphone and then sniffed the guts. "Yep, this is dead. But I think I may have one that will fit."

We walked out the back door and around to her squad car. Out to the east, the dog was digging away at a section of land that the firemen had excavated with their hoses.

"What is your dog doing?" she asked.

"He's digging at something."

"At what?"

"Who knows? Dogs do that kind of thing."

And then, only twenty feet away, the dog wrenched out a black tube from the ground and all the air gushed out of my lungs.

"Is that a hose?" Mary asked.

"I don't think so."

"We should check."

"It's just a piece of tubing. There were farmers here before me."

"Well, you don't want him eating that do you?"

Mary took a step across the driveway. We were close enough so the glue sealing the end of the tube shut could be seen. Apparently, the wrong kind of glue had been used because it was already starting to peel off the tube.

"He does it all the time. It's that non-toxic kind of agricultur- al tubing that was popular during the sixties. Besides, I just try and let dogs do their dog things, I mean, who are we to inter- vene?"

"Okay," she said and shrugged.

We went out to her car and in the passenger seat Mary had a big black bag. She had a small plastic case with a dozen batteries in it.

"What do you use all those batteries for?" I asked.

"Maybe I'll tell you one day." She selected one and fit it into the back of my cellphone. The digits lit up on the front panel. Mary handed me back the phone and as she did her fingers slipped over my palm. "Does your phone have a number?"

"I etched it in on the back."

"What is it?"

I turned the phone over.

"I'll call you," she said.

"Why not?"

"We could talk about your reviews."

"All right."

"Can you get me one?"

I went back inside the house and scanned the jungle of paper. I selected one from a slightly left of centre magazine that had no pornographic reviews that month and took it out to Mary. She held out her hand and accepted the rolled up paper.

"Bon appetit," I said.

She smiled, kissed the end of the newspaper and struck me on the shoulder with it.

The smell of burned sage folded over the road as Mary's blonde head turned and ducked into the squad car and all the yellow flowers of the bitter bush and pink prairie cacti opened to the sun even as the dog dug out the last of the tubing and tried to drag it back to the house.

THEN ON A SUNDAY it was true: I had been in love many times but had never been loved back. And so after emptying my pockets in front of those who did not know me, I realized there was nothing left to give. I did what anyone in this small town would do in such an event: I went to the Royal Tyrrell Museum of Paleontological History.

Churches, museums, and monuments like Stonehenge and perhaps even pornographic theatres are built for certain reasons and that is because people believe. And here, people really believe. They come loaded down with notebooks, diaries, trilobites and the faith of geologic epochs. They mutter on the mystery of the iridium line, the ecstasy of permineralization, and leave the horror of extinction by the door. Sometimes, they just try to forget what ails them.

They keep their heads raised, as if to the heavens, admiring varnished skulls and polished vertebrae. They awe over stuffed flora and petrified fauna. To be certain, there are those who came here by accident or because a tour brochure had said to do so when the golf courses were closed, but they are invisible and pass like ghosts through the tiled walls and well-preserved ancestors.

In the geologic science centre that is situated directly before the first huge dinosaur skeleton, I played with the sedimentary marble game where you churn a bunch of balls up and watch them settle according to their colour so you can see how the past covers things up in a very precise kind of order. Then I learned the difference in leverage between a beak and a jaw by manipulating a chrome set of calipers and came to understand why some animals thrived while others perished. But of course this was all foreplay, because the moment you walk around the next corner into a dark amphitheater, a huge petrified skull gazes down upon you from the top of a twenty-foot frame. The Albertosaurus stretched out his tiny hands and his hollow eye sockets are filled with hunger. And although the beast is long dead, it could still snatch up a victim at any second. At that moment a young boy ran around the corner and shouted, "There HE is. There he is!" like this was the one and only Albertosaurus in the world.

The young boy stood by in wonder with his arms raised in supplication and right then, something rumbled in my pocket. At first, I thought I had backed into a museum display that was shorting out, but nothing was near me. The object vibrated again and I couldn't remember sticking any battery operated sex toys in my clothes, although I know this is a common fetish of the voyeuristically inclined. I suppose it was possible a bee could have come in through the double glass doors and gone down my shirt. The blooming sage out front attracts them by the thousands. Maybe even a giant insect had been resurrected from the Badlands' past through some misdeed of cloning and had found its way into my pocket. I fumbled through my clothes and pulled out the cell-phone. It played a little tune and a light went on and the whole body convulsed as if it were having some kind of seizure.

"Aren't you going to answer that?" a woman beside me asked.

I punched a number of buttons on the front and a variety of tones came from the machine. Finally it stopped, although I had no idea why, or really what had made it erupt in the first place. No sooner had I put the phone back in my pocket when it started to ring again. A line of sweat broke out across my forehead and then above me, the giant Albertosaurus moved his stone head over, as if he was gazing down in pity on this lost soul and let his petrified mouth creep up just an inch in irony. I started for the door. I pressed a combination of number signs and red squares on the phone and just as I got free of the museum, the phone sputtered out and shut up again.

The cacti in the Badlands bit through my shoes and the walls of the coulees grew steep and narrow until the museum vanished into the background. In a while I was down a small creek bed with only a tiny wedge of flat mud in the bottom. Mosquitoes and blackflies rose from the slough in funnels that looked like tiny tornadoes and soon even the sounds from the highway were gone. Creosote from an old fence post brushed off my leg and a chunk of petrified wood rolled down the layered sandstone walls. My throat became very sore, as if a terrible flu was on the way or someone had strangled me with a leather belt so there was no voice left.

Down in the Badlands there are many remnants of the past: a

roll of duct tape, mosquito repellant, school yearbooks, a tube of lip gloss without a cap, and a leather satchel with a soiled magazine inside, a safety pin, and a black wrist watch with one strap missing. Not that it's a junkyard, but rather a cemetery. There was a green datebook and a tie clip, the tip of a fishing rod and a bookmark sticking out of the mud, and an old dog collar, too. Under a chunk of fossilized oyster I found a rusted shell cartridge, probably an old military issue and at that moment, the phone started going off again.

A rusted spade with a box handle rested against a roll of cattle wire. In a moment, the spade was in my hand and I opened a great trench in the soft mud of the August creek. I dropped the ringing phone into the hole and covered up the hole with dirt and cottonwood twigs and sage and grey rocks so the secrets of the Cretacea would stay down in the earth with the ancient beasts who knew them best.

ONE ON ONE

THE LAST TIME I saw Trisha we were supposed to get together for some noose-play. The format was usually the same. I'd go over to her place. She'd drag out in her slutty leather dress, black stilettos, and rubber top. We'd smoke a joint then have a glass of wine and pretty soon the porn would roll out: *Gallows Girls*, *Date with the Hangman*, or else some strangulation clips she'd pieced together from various horror movies and put onto a CD.

Once she got high she'd moan and that was my cue. I'd strip down naked and get on my knees. Trish would tie me up and walk around the room with her heels clicking on the hardwood floor. Then she'd examine my physique like it was a laboratory specimen, pull out the rope from her cedar chest, and prepare the noose with painful precision. She was into detail. Either I'd end up by choking out right away or else she'd toss the other end of the rope over a ceiling beam. Either-or, it was lights and sirens all the way.

I'd been into asphyxia as long as I can remember, probably way back into childhood. My first memory of sexual excitement was watching the hanging scene in *Cat Ballou* when Jane Fonda gets noosed and then rubbing my crotch on the shag carpet of our living room floor.

Transsexuals were something I was never really into. Not that I knew of, anyway. Sure, I'd seen them in porn magazines but in small town Alberta we didn't have many working in grocery stores. Finding women who were into kinky stuff was a pretty tall order and I was tired of dating columns, web sites, and tennis games that ended in agricultural discussions. Beggars couldn't be choosers. Pro-dommes were okay, but you had to drive all the way into Calgary for that. They charged a lot of money and came with their own set of troubles.

On the last Sunday of every month the Black Rhino Pub and Western Grill had a costume night and most of the kinky folk in the Red Deer valley went there under the guise of "dressing up." No one else drank on a Sunday night in our town so management posted a cover charge and let us do what we wanted. The owners begrudgingly enforced a dress code that kept the soldiers from Suffield at bay.

The first time I saw Trish I thought she was a girl. She leaned over the bar with a champagne cocktail and had on a black mini skirt, white blouse, and blue wig. She was beautiful really, too much makeup, but stunning. Lithe, thick-lipped, something you'd expect to see on that old British television series UFO where all the space-women had big boobs, blue hair, and Lycra spacesuits.

"That's nice hair," I said.

"Thank you," she said back.

Up close you could tell: Adam's apple, strong hands and a voice pitched halfway in the wrong direction, but by then I was already in far too deep to back out.

Talking kink to strangers was fair game at the Rhino. Essentially that's why people went even though most of them were wannabes. Small talk was just a waste of time.

"What are you into?" I asked her.

"Role play," she said. "Breath control, asphyxia. I like scenes with a beginning, middle, and end. You know, narrative."

Then she giggled and bit on her string of white pearls. If there had been a lightning rod outside, I would have been fried. This was the grand prize, the Lotto Max. Well, maybe the Lotto Mini Max because the pure gold would have been a woman, but what the hell this was good. What she had between her legs simply didn't matter.

"Fabulous," I said. "Do you like noose-play?"

"Oh yes. I used to watch westerns when I was a teenager. My mother thought I was into horses."

"I think we'll get on."

Trish sized me up, considered her options, then glanced around at the competition. The bar was filled with a number of overweight oil riggers, some obviously disturbed kinksters with prosthetic limbs, and a few newbies who looked very nervous. The men outnumbered the women, the women called the shots, and most people's idea of kink in the Red Deer valley was doing missionary in the barn.

"You don't mind?" She held up her cocktail and stared at the olive so the sentence didn't need to be finished.

"You're gorgeous."

Her eyelashes fluttered. Her gold fingernail circled the rim of her glass.

"You've done a T-Girl before?"

"Sure," I lied. "Had playmates in Calgary. Pretty low-key there. You don't see many cross-dressers at the Stampede."

She laughed. I got a drink. The bartender stood on the other side of his fence expressionless. He had been given strict instructions by the management to stay non-judgmental, shut up, and collect the tabs.

"Have you played with anyone here?" she asked.

Okay, I'd gotten to know a few friends here. Sal, the blonde who was drinking scotch at the One-Armed Bandit, I dated but that didn't work out. Sal liked ponies way too much. Jen, a tall brunette in her fifties, stood by the jukebox in her rubber suit. Architect by trade, she was into flogging, which I liked, but she was looking for a husband and I wasn't. Tom and Terry were gay. Not that that bothered me. They liked to talk about rodeos and came to the club together because this was the only place in town they could act natural. Pam, a woman my age with red hair, walked past us and lifted her glass. She was athletic, into just about anything, but she was also the most sought after commodity in the circuit, knew it, and so I didn't bother. I'd been down that road before.

"Nothing serious," I said. "Pam's okay to look at but that's it."

"Trouble."

"Really?"

"I mean I've got nothing against her personally, but there's a lot of estrogen flying around in that chassis."

"Bi?"

"Mm," Trish said. "Drama queen. The lengths she'll go to are unbelievable."

"Whatever."

The evening wore on and somewhere around Tom Collins number four it dawned on me that Trisha's real name was Tad and he worked in the Chamber of Commerce. Great looking guy but I'd only ever seen him from a distance and, besides, at the club you didn't talk about what went on in vanilla life. Rule 1(a): No blabbing. I checked my watch.

"What do you think?" I said.

She bit her pearls again and stared at the ceiling.

"Do you want to go to my place?"

I waited the compulsory one-point-five seconds.

"All right," I said.

"Me topping you. Me on top all the way since it's our first time."

"Sure."

This was an absolutely ludicrous thing to consent to. Going to a complete stranger's house by yourself and being on the receiving end of some very dangerous technical work was not a street-smart decision. There are probably stats on how many people die each year with ropes around their necks, but I didn't care. I convinced myself that her deference rendered her harmless. Saying I was so big and strong that I had to be on the bottom. And then it just didn't matter. I took her hand and we walked to the front door. Her shoulder smelled of lime. All the would-be perverts in the bar eyed us with needy condescension and Trish gave someone in the corner a screw-you wave.

Trish's house was a wartime bungalow on the industrial side of the tracks. Lots of creosote, railway ties, and abandoned grain silos. The stucco was grey and the sidewalk patiently cracked. Out front there was a bed of weeds and a lonely thistle garden. She drove her truck around back and parked down the alley that was encased in caragana.

"Neighbours," she said. "There's just no point in parking out front."

The inside of the house was sparse and lonely. A couch, a cold hardwood floor, and a couple of black books on the shelf detailing public planning policy. We went straight downstairs. Downstairs was where the action happened. Downstairs was it. Teak floor, big screen TV, air ionizer, full spectrum lighting and a couple of tell-tale hooks hanging from the beams that couldn't be used for potted plants. The door to the playroom had a window in it and also a lock.

"I cook upstairs," she said. "This is where I live."

She turned on the lights, closed the curtain, and leaned back on her IKEA sofa.

"Joint?" she said.

"Why not?"

Trish lit up. Hard to tell if her tits were implants or falsies. Didn't matter. The cold hardness of desire swept over her face and she stretched her long legs on a pillow. Her makeup made her look Oriental.

"Strip for me," she said.

Part of the kinkster game is you can do all kinds of over-the-top stuff and get away with it. Stuff that would get you thrown out of a grade eight drama class is prime time here. I stripped down and stood straight out, pounding, aching, stretching, and making all the air in the basement reek of testosterone. Then I got down on my knees and kissed her shoes. The skin on her calf was tanned and amazingly smooth. Somewhere in the last thirty seconds she had lost her nylons. She got up, walked around behind me, and tied my hands behind my back with a hair dryer cord. Then she pulled a thick cotton rope out from a cedar chest and bit on the end. I got all the technical details of the rope's weight, diameter, hemp content, and load limit. I'll never forget her made-up face absolutely perfect in want, the black pupils searching deep and insect like into a need of mine no one else had ever seen. She fastened one end of the rope around the beam in a half-hitch and the other around my neck. Then she pulled up her dress. Champagne bubbles burst in my head, my throat filled with salt, and an alarm clock went off as my skull hit the floor.

"How was that?" she said after. She lounged on the sofa with another cocktail and her toenails had pink lilies painted on them.

"Fabulous."

"I think I'll keep you."

The next day, I saw Pam in the bank. I knew she was going to break a cardinal rule of the club but she strolled up to the cheque writing counter and stood way too close to be anything but sexual.

"How did it go last night?" she said.

I gave her a blank stare. She had a yellow rodeo scarf wrapped around her neck like a lot of tourists did in the middle of the summer and cowboy boots that probably hadn't been out of their box in years.

"Fine."

"I'm sorry I didn't get a chance to talk to you last night," she said. "Didn't want to interrupt. Got time for lunch?"

"I guess."

"Why have you been ignoring me?"

This seemed to be pretty much a law of the kink universe. You'd spend years looking for people in solitude, going to stupid socials, attending workshops, answering ads, and nothing, nada, nyet, then all of a sudden you got lucky and everybody wanted a chip of the action. We went over to the Big Horn for a Bronto burger and got a booth. Pam smelled of lilac perfume, something French anyway. She had delicate features, a small nose, and in the daylight her hair was the same colour as a barn on fire. She held her fingers up in an okay sign as she ate so she wouldn't get mayo on the table and quizzed me about my nocturnal encounter.

"I didn't take you for the bi type," she said.

"I'm not."

She gave me a sallow look and asked for another Pepsi.

"Please," she said.

"Trish and I just have a lot in common."

"Uh-huh."

"She's a nice lady."

Pam raised an eyebrow and agreed on the pronoun according to protocol.

"I guess I just know the other side of her," she said.

"Which side?"

"The Tad side."

I shrugged. Like I fucking cared.

"You've done the plastic bag routine with her?" she asked.

I dished out the "gentlemen don't tell" smile.

Pam wasn't giving up. She wanted content. Some of the mayo stuck to her chin and she made a point of shoving her index finger down her throat to clean it up.

"She likes the One Hour Martinizing bags because they cling," she said.

"Really."

"But she plays rough. Don't get me wrong, I like rough."

The words lingered for a dramatically long time. "In fact, I like almost everything. Watching, too. But look after yourself. Have a good fail-safe system in place is all I can say."

She took a menthol cigarette out of her purse, tapped the end on the tabletop, but didn't light up. A sign above the door said No Smoking. $200.00 fine.

"Are you a pro?" I said.

"A what?"

"A Pro-domme." Calling someone a whore was rude but a Pro-domme had a ring of aristocracy. "I mean not at this minute, but at some time in the past? You just have that air about you."

What I was actually saying in code was you are being a bitch, but Pam didn't take the bait.

"Can you play tennis?" she said.

"Yes. Of course I can play tennis."

"No, I mean can you really play? Are you any good? Not can you put on a pair of white shorts and look smart. It's tough finding good players around here. All the guys want to do is cattle rope and they get their dicks stuck in the net."

"I'm good," I said.

"Up for a game some time?" She studied her unlit cigarette. Her red nails were perfectly manicured. "Just tennis. That's all I'm looking for. I know you're taken."

"Sure," I said.

"You don't mean that."

"I do."

"Ten bucks a game?"

I went home and practiced against the wall. About three, the kink creep started inside me and all I could think about was Trish's tanned legs and fake Georgian accent. She worked at the bank until four, but I knew I couldn't go there. Didn't want to show up at her place unannounced and most certainly didn't want to wait until the end of next month to get done again. I wrote my name and number on a piece of paper and wedged it into her back door. Some hornets had made a nest beneath the soffit. By six the phone rang.

"Hey baby," she said.

"Hey," I said.

There's a point in any conversation when it becomes all about sex and we had already reached that point.

"What are you up to?" I said.

"Waiting for you."

"When?"

"Give me half an hour. I have to get made up." Then she paused. "Do you have a car?"

"Sure," I said.

"Can you pick up a prescription for me at the drugstore?"

"Of course."

"Then park out back, okay?"

When I went downstairs the air already reeked of hemp. Fleet-wood Mac was on the stereo and some very nasty porn was on the huge television. A nude man slicked down with oil was being garroted by a woman in a witch costume.

"Hey hon," the voice said from the off-suite.

"Hey," I said.

"What to wear to a hanging," Trish said and came out of the room in five-inch heels and a fishnet body suit. She wrapped her fingers over the door frame and I knew I wasn't going to have much say in what happened next.

A lot of the times I'd wake up the next day with a searing headache. My right eye would go out of focus. Rope burns too. I took to wearing high collar shirts to work which was stupid in the middle of July and everyone just assumed it was a hickey. One of the girls in the office kept giving me knowing grins. My short-term memory faltered, I'd been choked out four times in the past two weeks and I was pretty sure Trish was hot waxing me while I was under. I got used to the after-effects, but from time to time things got scary. Loud bells would go off in my head during hangings, shapes would flit by in the room so fast I couldn't make out what they were, and often I heard people laughing above me when I was collapsed on the floor.

"Was there someone else in the room last night?" I asked Trish.

"Who?"

"I have no idea, who?"

She shook her head. "I don't do that."

"I thought I could hear voices. Up above."

"That's pretty common," she said. We were watching a video from The House of Gaspers where a pretty blonde from Toronto wearing lace gloves strings a man up and pushes him off a stack of telephone books. "Do you want to stay the night?"

That came down like a thistle in a corn dog.

"Uh, no," I said. "Thanks, but I don't think so."

Trish put her hand on my knee.

"Okay," she shrugged.

PAM HAD BEAT me three sets in a row and it was thirty degrees in the shade, which there was none of. She had on a white tennis top, white dress and one of those sweatbands around her head that people wear on Viagra commercials. Basically she was a poster girl for any Ivy League college in the country and I owed her thirty bucks.

"Give up?" she said.

"No, but I have to go."

"Where?"

"Got a date."

I bent over to pick up a stray ball and she struck me on the ass with the racket.

"You two spend a lot of time together," she said.

"Do we?"

"You spend the night, don't you?"

It wasn't a question.

"Not often," I said.

"Really?"

"That kind of stuff isn't for me."

"Don't tell me," she said. "You're just in it for the sex."

"Aren't you?"

Pam went over and leaned against her red Volvo. Her skin was dark and covered in sweat.

"Yes," she said. She opened the trunk and pulled out an ice sack. Inside there were two orange popsicles and she handed me one. "What's on the agenda for today? If *you* can be so blunt."

"Not sure," I said. "Too rough for you, anyway."

"Doubt that."

"Mm."

"No," she said. "Call him."

"She'll say no."

"He'll say yes. He always does."

"Not today."

She opened the car door, took out her cell phone and tossed it to me.

"I know what you do and I know Tad. Call him."

I dialed the number and waited.

"Hey, hon," she said.

"Hey, listen. I'm running a bit behind. Got to have a shower."

"Come over sweaty. I like sweaty hunks. We can do a medieval scene."

"Not this sweaty. Give me half an hour."

"I'll be ready when you get here," she said.

Pam examined the threads on her racket then looked up.

"Hey, listen," I said. "Is it all right if Pam comes over?"

"Pam?"

"She said she wanted to watch and that she knows what we do. I don't know if you'd be into that or not."

Trish thought for a long time.

"Whatever," she said.

We had a shower at my place and Pam made a point of leaving the door open when she got wet. Everything that wasn't freckles on that girl was red; lips, nipples, hair, even eyes when the bathroom light hit them the right way. Then she talked me into a scotch and soda and after we stuffed our tennis clothes into the trunk because she said she'd dryclean them for me. On the way over she gave me a litany of her asphyx experiences, which sounded canned, but the oil she'd smeared on her legs sparkled diamonds in the sun and I made a wrong turn at Trisha's street.

"Better park around back," she said.

"You know the routine, do you?"

"I know."

I had this scene replaying in my head of Pam screwing me while I was choked out and knocked over a garbage can. The cottonwoods were drooping and covered in dust. The back alley hadn't seen another car in days. We walked across the unkempt yard. The grass was long and yellow. A birdhouse once painted red was sun-worn to off-pink.

"She needs to do some yardwork," I said.

"Too many hormones," Pam said.

"Hormones?"

"They cut down on your desire to complete tasks."

"Never had that problem with me."

"Don't shoot your load too fast, okay? I want to have some fun."

We got up to the door and I had this bad feeling she might just mean screwing vanilla-style so I said, "Are you sure you're into this?"

"Relax," she said. "You have no idea. Don't sweat it. It'll all be good."

But as soon as we got inside we both knew it wasn't all good. A fan circling above the lonely dining room table made no noise. The air was stagnant. There was one plate, one teacup, and one napkin. No stereo, no porn playing, no sounds of Trish clicking her shoes or buckling up the chrome latches on her leather corset.

"Trish?" I called out, no answer. "Hey hon, you ready yet?"

I realized I'd called her hon. Pam shuffled her purse between her palms checked the fridge and we went down the stairs. A newspaper from August, 1945 had been stuffed in the wall for insulation. At the playroom, the door was locked. Pam's face seized up. I'd seen that panic in wheat buyers' eyes right before they knew the market was going to crash and I gazed through the window.

Trish was buckled down on her knees with the rope cinched around her neck. Her face was white as a mannequin and her dress was pulled down to her thighs. Something shriveled and pink had caught in the zipper.

Pam looked away for half a second and I panicked for a knife or anything to cut Trish down with. I was just about to pick up a screwdriver from the end table when Pam grabbed my arm.

"What are you doing?" she said.

"Cutting her down."

"Don't go in there," Pam said. "Jesus, she's been dead for an hour."

Not much doubt about that. The face utterly plastic, bloodless and strangely masculine stretched beneath the blue wig.

"We've got to do something," I said.

"Like what?"

"Call someone."

"Not here," she said. She put a finger to her lip. "We'll go down to the pay phone and call."

"Are you out of your mind?"

Pam was whispering in a loud hoarse voice which was louder than if she'd been just talking.

"No, I'm very much in my mind. Not all my blood is in my dick. Listen to me and listen good. There's no need for us to get tangled up here. She's dead. I'm sorry for it but don't want to spend the next five days answering a bunch of questions from the medical examiner and half-a-hundred cops."

"We can't just leave."

"I am. You are too. Don't touch anything. We'll walk out the back door back to my car and leave. Nobody will even know we were here. Don't be stupid."

We walked out of the room, shut the door and walked through the caragana bushes. My mouth tasted of ash. In the small town dust bowl that was Trish's neighbourhood only a magpie saw us ditch the screwdriver in a grain silo that had been deserted since 1953.

Pam made me stop the car at the 7-Eleven because I was too shaky to drive. When there was no one around, she went to the phone booth and dialed the police non-emergency line. She took a piece of tinfoil from her purse and put it over the receiver.

"Hi," she said. "I'm calling from out of town. I'm just in visiting. I got a phone call from a relative who's got a lot of psychological problems. He didn't sound right. Can you go and check on him? Nothing serious probably, but he has a history."

She gave the address and then hung up. We drove to the tennis court and put on our sweaty, stinking whites and played tennis for the rest of the afternoon, and more than a few people saw us there batting the ball around and laughing and commented on what a handsome couple we were.

MY DAUGHTER OF THE DEAD REEDS

HIS DAUGHTER WAS dead, he told me, drowned in the river. Claimed by the tope clay and fouled cattle wire of the Red Deer River basin, she would never surface. Come Monday morning her classroom desk would be empty and a pair of ballet shoes would hang unclaimed in the cupboard and no one would help. How can you turn down a plea like that? How can you say no to a man crying on your front step with his cuffs turned up like he never made it past the third grade?

"You'd better come in."

"She was wearing a bright-pink sweater and rubber boots." He came in and there were reeds on his feet and they stuck to my floor. "I told her not to go along the river. But she did anyway. She's got a set of brass bells around her wrist that tinkle like Christmas toys so we can't miss her."

"Where is your wife?"

"She's retarded." He threaded the rim of his hat through his hands and tossed it aside. "She's retarded and she doesn't understand. Not tonight, anyway."

"Haven't you told her?"

"She's off her meds."

She was simple, I knew that. I knew a little. She came to a few of my parties. She had problems with the complicated things in life—area codes, traffic circles, and long grocery lists—but I wouldn't have called her retarded. So I let him in. He sat on the couch. He was cold and he had on a scarlet vest and hip waders from the Salvation Army, but I let him in anyway.

He didn't like my place much. I am a bachelor. I live alone. I live with the petrified skeletons of ancient Badland creatures that I put together for a hobby and that sort of thing is against his religion. Fossils are popular here. They're not a bad hobby. They don't mean you're derelict or anti-social or have disregard for other people's beliefs, but he sat between the calcified bones and his eyes flitted from femur to cranium and tried to pretend they didn't exist.

I handed him a glass of brandy and felt a little bad for it. He's a religious man who has lost his daughter and all I did was give him liquor. But he rolled down the brandy in one shot and didn't even wince. Maybe there were things I didn't know. The more time goes on, the more I realize I do not know, like the production of pins or the evolution of Mesozoic flowers.

"Have you told the police?" I asked.

"Why?"

"So they can help us look for her."

"They won't."

"What do you mean they won't? That's their job."

"She has to be gone twenty-four hours."

"No. That's not right. How old is she?"

"She's seven." He nodded. He shut his eyes and counted the

years. Maybe he was counting something else, too. "No, wait. She's eight."

"Eight? They don't wait a whole day to go looking for an eight-year-old who's missing in the river."

"They will with her."

"Why?"

He shrugged. "She's done it before."

"That is ridiculous. Call them now. I know one of the sergeants."

"Do you have a phone?"

I didn't. I do not like things electronic. They are scabied. They are horsehair. They get in the way of the real things in life. Real things are bones. Real things are beasts. Real things are proving the past and rye, and drinking with women late into the night and then having them naked on top of you, braids up and down, growling. People spend all day long on cellphones, BlackBerrys, and computers and don't even know what the insides of their kitchens look like so I don't bother with them.

"Even we have a phone," he said.

"Let's walk down to the station."

"It won't do any good."

"They have all the proper tools for a search. They have ropes. They have maps and infrared. They'll make it easier."

"You have lights and ropes," he said.

That was true enough. Outside, the sun died orange and sent a long shadow across my workbench just to prove his point.

"Besides," he said. "We've been through this before with them. They want to look in the house first. They want photographs. They want to ask my wife questions."

"So let them."

"No. She'll screw things up. There's always an excuse. They'll never look in the right places."

"What are the right places?"

He did not answer. He sat between a spilled glass of wine and a discarded pair of woman's nylons from a weekend party and stared into my vacant living room. There are a few other things you should know about my living room. It is large. It has high ceilings. Only one couch and one chair. No television. Hardwood floors and no carpet. Along with the fossils there are also remnants of gatherings that happened too near in the past to be fossils. Stains. Smudges. Stilettos. A calendar girl with a blue bikini, a singles magazine soaked with merlot, and a leather-bound address book with many names. He stared out across this smear of a house and the stubble on his chin grew dull.

"Why do you do all this?" he said.

"I like to imagine how those creatures used to be. I know, your religion, you don't believe in evolution."

"I'm not talking about the fossils," he said.

And then he put his head in his hands and he howled. He howled so loud his voice went down into my basement and rattled the jars of preserved plums, and the tiny skeleton of a bird encased in formaldehyde trembled, too.

"Don't make me go out there by myself," he said. "I know you don't have children so you can't understand, but please help me find the only thing I've ever loved."

"All right," I said and made my way to the workbench where all the tools of the trade were kept. "I'll help you find her."

Was this a bad thing? Was this a pernicious thing? Did I say yes because I just wanted to shut him up? Maybe I deferred because his wife was promiscuous. She went to parties, that much I knew.

She didn't connect well at soirees but it was obvious what she wanted. It was obvious what she wasn't getting at home although I never went there. She would stand there in the corner of a kitchen with a wool skirt hiked up to her knees and a single malt clenched against her ribs. I think her nose was pierced.

We went down to the Red Deer River in the dark. Let me tell you something about the Red Deer River at night. The water is slow and sullen and hides things in the filigreed shadows of cottonwood. It hides alabaster larvae and cardamom condoms; stories of pioneers starving on the banks, of soldiers who went away to distant European wars and never came back. Today, there are stories of automated farming accidents and postmodern suicides because it's such a melancholy place, the pastel grey Badlands sunk below the prairie with spent drilling rigs and abandoned wheat kings. But sometimes people just kill themselves because economic times are bad or they have nowhere else to go. They could have done it in Calgary or Vancouver, but this is a better place for it.

I had the flashlights attached to our helmets. The kind spelunkers used. You could fall in the river with them and the bulbs would still work. Still find the clutches of ancient Pteranodons and the tangle of teeth in the late-night sediment. I ran my hand across a layer of prehistoric rock that vanished into the water. Lacerated by the glaciers, the ridges coughed up Cretaceous spines and amber wings.

"Forget about those," he said. "Give me one of those lights and turn them on."

"Why are we looking here?"

"This is the way she always comes."

Laid waste in the mud was the axle of a combine, a weasel skull, and what could have been a freebase pipe.

"Isn't it dangerous this way?"

"Yes," he said. "Of course."

"Then why do you let her do it?"

"Children are like that," he said. "You tell them not to do something, but they go ahead and do it anyway."

His face was dirty. He looked like a miner with my headlamp on. His breath came out in a white cloud then hung around in a bundle.

"Maybe we should retrace her steps," I said. "What school did she come from?"

"School?"

"Yes, what grade school?"

"I'm not sure."

"How can you not be sure?"

"You bring your dates here, don't you?" was all he said.

There was a kite hung up in the willow. An orange kite with red poppies and a crepe tail like a child would have. In the dark sky between the branches there were other things, too. Underwear and plastic bags, lottery tickets and soiled rags. Beer boxes and plastic ashtrays, relics from unhappy cupboards. Anything that wasn't wanted elsewhere wound up here.

Then in the soft mud by some caragana roots he spotted a set of footprints with the chevron pattern still stamped into the silt. The trail came out of the aspen grove and then meandered along the water, left by a small person who was not at all in a hurry.

"Those are hers," he said. "Those are her boots. I know them. I put them on her this morning. There's a chunk of heel missing."

I got down on my knees. The harsh light fell across the track and on the right foot, and sure enough, the back half of the heel was gone, the rubber cracked and ragged. The trail of boot prints wandered through a cluster of reeds and with each step, they changed a little. The toes sharpened, the chevrons became scaly, and the heels narrowed into claws. By the irrigation flue, the tracks were clustered in panic like a child hopelessly lost and knowing so and then they entered the river and were gone.

"What do you see?" he said.

"Nothing."

"You're lying."

"A sign that says phosphates must not exceed ten parts per million."

"That's not what I mean. You're an expert on tracks. What do they say?"

"These tracks aren't new. They're ancient."

"Stop that. I'm tired of hearing about your non-existent fossils. She's been taken into the water right here," he said. He waded into the river and ran back and forth like a dog that couldn't decide where to cross.

"She hasn't gone into the water," I said.

By the mouth of an oxbow pond where the silt lay deep, a coil of barbwire ran from an old cattle fence and was fouled at mid-current. Trapped beneath the surface, a knot of hunchback clothes bobbled up and down and because the fabric was pink, I pulled on the wire. The weight sank back. Not like a fighting fish. Not like a salmon or even the dead pull of a codfish, but a fiction that belonged on the river bottom forever. I remember once, as a boy, I went fishing in our boat with my father and uncle. We were out on the deep salt water and the rod bent down in an arc. My father and my uncle spent an hour reeling the cargo in and then a bloated dark coil welled up to the surface, and just as the limb touched the stern of the boat, my father said, go inside.

Now my father and uncle are gone and this is a river, not the ocean. But out of the back eddy rose the drowned tangle of soaked wool and rubber boots. The body was small and childish, the limbs knotted in reeds and the blonde hair strewn with petroleum from the very centre of the earth. Mutilated by the cattle wire, the skull had been stretched into a wedge and around the neck there was still a string of brass bells.

My neighbour threw his arms around the carcass and the head lobbed back. The eyes were baby blue, but the beak was triangular and the arms scaly, reptilian wings.

"My Angela," he said.

"What are you doing?"

"She's still breathing."

He put his mouth over the beak, exposed the red gums and razor teeth and blew until the meager chest inflated. I grabbed him by the shoulder and struck him in the face.

"Stop it."

"How can you say that?" There was blood on his lips and on the sand.

"It is not your daughter."

I cut off the barbed coils with a pair of pliers. The wings flopped apart in an arc of crude oil. Rolled out, the span was six feet. The eye sockets were filled with vitreous humour that had soured in death and the claws on its feet had punctured the rubber boots like ivy grown through concrete.

"We have to bury her," he said. He kissed the leather jaw and did up the blue buttons on the dress. "We have to bury her and give her something proper."

"We have to call the museum," I said.

"Museum? How can you say my daughter belongs in a museum?"

"That is not your daughter."

"She's not an animal, she's not something to be shot with formaldehyde and stuffed in a jar. She's a human being."

"All right, we have to call the medical examiner then," I said.

"No," he said. "They'll just take her away. It would be like everything else. They'd just take her away and then I'd never see her again."

This was long past reason. The dead creature's eye gazed into the stark splinters of poplar night to a place where there was no family and no dawn.

"We have to take her home," he said. He had thought this out. "We'll take her home and we'll put her there on the kitchen table until it's time. That's where all children go. That's the way it should be. We'll burn frankincense and pray. Then I'll find a minister and we'll have a service. In the churchyard, the steepled one behind the train tracks. You'll come, won't you? I want you to come. You're the only one who will come, no one else will. You'll have to be with me when I tell my wife. I can't do it alone. She'll die. She'll crumple in grief."

Then he wrapped his hand around the tiny set of claws that extruded from the wing and squeezed them. Balled inside the fingers was a coil of kite string.

RUSSELL FAIRBANKS HAD slipped on the front deck of a Massey Ferguson combine and fell down into the blades. His leg was severed at the knee and his femoral artery was punctured in not one but two places. He was rushed to the hospital and I cannot recall if he lived or if he died because his parents were religious and would not allow a blood transfusion. I remember Lilly Carmine died of frostbite and her parents looked for her everywhere, but someone else found her inside an old latrine. Perhaps they were secular.

I thought about these things as I walked up the steps to his house. My neighbour stayed in the back of the pickup truck with his waterlogged corpse. He kept whispering, "My little fallen fruit," and there was no chance I'd be wading back through that. There are two ways to rationalize a criminal act. One is to say that it is not criminal, that it is for the greater good. Like a crusade or starting a war. Perhaps keeping a handgun at home. The other is to embrace the criminality and eat your young. I knocked on the door and straightened my collar.

His wife was standing in the sparse living room smoking Virginia Slims with her heel hooked on a coiled hot water heater. She watched the ceiling fan turn. She wore silver bangles on her ankles and her legs were tanned. The room smelled of lemon pledge.

"Oh, it's you," she said.

I closed the door. On the table was a gin fizz and a set of earrings.

"Are you all right?" I said.

"Why wouldn't I be?" She pointed at a silver tray that held crystal decanters: bourbon, scotch and rye.

"You've no clue what's going on?"

"With him?" she said. "I'm adjusting."

She turned to the fireplace and twisted a portrait of a small child around to reflect the light from the kitchen chandelier.

"Is that her?" I said.

"Who?"

"Your daughter."

She wasn't listening. She stared into the glass for a moment

CRETACEA & OTHER STORIES

and then glossed her lips with cherry balm. The portrait was a five-by-eight black-and-white photo of a small girl with blonde hair on a swing set.

"I think I took it better than he did," she said. "He's always been the soft one. He's always been the one that in the end couldn't handle loss. *For all the loves we know, death makes us fonder.* That might be Shakespeare. Or maybe it's Hunter S. Thompson. Who knows?"

"What are you going to do now?"

"Do? I'm going out," she said.

"You might want to hang around."

"Why?"

"He's outside."

"What's he done this time?" She scooped up the earrings and pushed the portrait back into place so the glass reflected her lobes. "It's ridiculous, isn't it? But I have to use it. He doesn't tolerate mirrors. He says they're vain. It's got something to do with the Book of Daniel. Is there anything going on at your place tonight?"

"No."

"Why not?"

"Because I was just out with your husband in the river. We're both soaking wet."

"In the river?" She stopped and examined the gin. She declined. Perhaps there was something better down the road. "Whatever for?"

"Listen, he dragged this thing out of the water. You might want to have a look."

"What kind of thing?"

"I'm not sure. It's grotesque, really."

"Just give me the synopsis, okay?"

She walked over to the picture window and let some ashes drop into a chrome tray. The ashes fluttered down like owls and I thought for a moment she might lick one up.

"Well, you're going to find out," I said. "He's bringing it inside."

"Figures," she said. "Maybe I'll go over to Jamieson's. He's a bourbon drinker. They've got friends in from the West Coast. Why don't you come along?"

"Not tonight."

She opened her mouth a little and the smoke crept out. She reached over and adjusted my lapel. She picked off a reed.

"Why not?" she said.

"I'm not up to it."

"That's too bad. I need to get away. Look, he hasn't told me much," she said. She shrugged. "I'm leaving. He's keeping the house. I don't care. I don't want it. In case you haven't noticed he's not the greatest with words. Besides, I don't tell him every-thing, do I?"

There was a sick mutton feeling in the room. The floor had gone gritty with the silt my boots had dragged in from the river and between my teeth there was a dirty feeling too. She reached out and rested the end of her cigarette an inch away from my Adam's apple then teased me by drooping the ember closer.

"Where is your daughter?" I said.

"What?"

"Where is your young daughter right now, I mean is she at relatives or out lawn bowling or drinking Jack Daniel's or in her room sleeping or what?"

"I have not a clue what you're talking about."

"Who is this portrait of?"

She picked the framed photo off the mantel. The girl sat on the swing with a trace of sepia melancholy on her lips.

"I have no idea," she said.

"Where is the photo from?"

"He cut it out of a Sears catalogue, I think."

"He said your daughter was drowned in the river."

"Is that what he told you?"

She sucked on her cigarette with her thumb under her chin. She was nodding, gazing off to the ceiling, perhaps at the crepe paper chickens, perhaps at the jar of cashews. Not at all at the photograph. The young girl was wearing boots and bells around her neck, dressed up and delicate as if her parents were shipping her off to an event that she was too young to understand.

OPEN SOIL

GARTNER LEANED TOO far over the gas pumps. It wasn't like he was trying to scare customers away, but he swung the fuel hose back and forth as if he might hit the next person who drove in.

"You do that on purpose, don't you?" Denise said. She stood there with a squeegee in one hand and a red rag in the other, waiting for the next car to arrive.

Gartner shrugged. He turned away and stared out across the Badlands. Up on the prairie, a few round bales dotted the hill and a tractor made its way across a field. He remembered a poem he had read in school about a farmer plodding his way home after working in the fields, but couldn't recall who wrote it.

"I don't know how you expect to do any business if you stand here threatening the customers." She put the squeegee back into the bucket and pulled down her ball cap to keep the sun out of her eyes. "Like it doesn't make any difference to me, you know. I just thought the place would be a little more interesting if someone actually came in and bought some antifreeze once in a while."

"You get paid anyway," he said, but by then she had made her way back to the station door and couldn't hear him.

The wind pushed a few blades of grass across the parking lot.

For September it was hot. The intersection was on one of the busiest in the Red Deer valley. The gas station was not. A lot of people came and went on their way to the museum. Everything was about dinosaurs now. Bronto burgers. Pterodactyl fries. Gartner shut his eyes. It was almost harvest. People were supposed to be happy around here when it was harvest. Or when the price of oil went up. He ran his hands over his face. His fingers smelled like gas, or kerosene; he didn't care much which. He hated the smell.

Denise went out by the road and pulled the big metal sign back off the driveway. For some reason it always ended up in the middle of the parking lot, halfway blocking traffic.

Inside, Gartner sat down at his desk. A wooden cuckoo bobbed back and forth on the sill. The bird drank from a little bowl of water and then the head bounced back up. As long as the bowl was full and the bird was in the sunlight, it would do it all day. It would do it forever, in fact. Gartner had spent the entire weekend filling the bowl up with water and keeping the cuckoo in the sun, just to see how long the bird could go on for. It never quit. He'd checked the inside of the bird for batteries once, but hadn't found any.

"Is this like perpetual motion?" he asked Denise when she came back inside.

"Perpetual motion doesn't exist. Perpetual motion would be if you had a closed system with no energy coming in and something kept on moving forever. This isn't it."

He wiped his hands on a rag. She'd be going back to school in a couple of days and he'd be alone at the station. Gartner figured she had everything going for her. Smart, good looks, hard working. She wore her hair tucked up under her baseball cap. A bunch of hair stuck out the back like a horse's tail and spilled onto her shoulders. He didn't really like the style, but what the hell, she seemed to.

"Your father called," she said. She flipped the calendar up. She was going to cross off another day with her magic marker, but then thought better of the idea.

"Really?"

"Or maybe your mother called on his behalf. Can't remember which."

"What did they want, collectively?"

"They just wanted to check on the ledger."

"The ledger?"

"They are, after all, the owners."

"Must be four o'clock," he said. His father checked every day at four o'clock. He took his boots off the desk and went over to the phone. He picked up the receiver and then put it down. "Why do you think all receivers are black?" he asked.

"They're not," she shrugged. "Like T-Fords. They can be any colour as long as it's black."

She laughed. Gartner figured he should laugh too, like this was something he was supposed to know, but he couldn't think what.

"Like Henry Ford," she said.

"Like Henry Ford," he said.

She reached into her pocket and pulled out a package of ciga-rettes. The moment she did, Gartner reached into his pocket and pulled out a shiny tin of chewing tobacco. But there was no tobacco inside. There was a pad of pressed wet clay. Gartner stuck his nose into the tin. The clay smelled damp and green like the rain in June and new grass. He remembered an old Chev truck he'd had and a girl named Julie, but wasn't quite clear what the connection was.

"Pavlov," Denise said and blew a ring of smoke up to the ceiling.

"What?"

He thought for the longest time. "So, perpetual motion. Nothing can go on forever. Like if you don't put anything into it."

"Pretty much," she said.

"Thank Christ," he nodded.

HE CLOSED THE gas station at nine, gave Denise a ride home and then drove home himself. Halfway home, he slowed down by the bakery and watched Patty slide stale bread off the shelves. She did the same thing every night. For a bakery, Gartner thought it was strange, because you couldn't actually see much bread through the glass. The window was engorged with flowers. Tulips, crocuses, ferns, palms, and even cacti. Red and white flowered ones, but none of the blue ones. Blue flowering cacti were pretty hard to find in these parts. Gartner had never been able to find a blue cactus in any of the books, but he was sure they were around somewhere.

He wondered if he ought to go in and buy a loaf. They'd be half price. She'd said to him once that she threw away a couple of loaves each night and it always hurt her to do so. She ought to take them down to the Salvation Army or food bank, she'd said. Problem was, there wasn't a Salvation Army or food bank in town, so out they went. She had shaken her head right when the word *hurt* came out of her mouth and Gartner could remember there had been the smell of dirt on the floor when she said the word. Not because the bakery was a dirty place, really. Just because it had been early spring with melting snow and someone had tracked mud in. He really ought to go in and buy a loaf. Then he remembered he had a dozen loaves frozen in the deep freeze that he would never eat and so he drove on.

Out on Gartner's front lawn, there were grasshoppers every-where. When he walked across the lawn they jumped out of his way. Denise had said she thought they were creepy. Insects hid-ing everywhere under your feet, flying up into the sky when people came along. There was something sinister about that. She said if there were an atomic war, only insects would survive, and grow to huge sizes, two or three feet long. Insects were sur-vivors, but their size was limited because they didn't have lungs. Two or three feet was about their limit. Denise said she had nightmares about insects.

He got down on his knees and searched for one of the grasshoppers, but they were too fast for him. He put his nose to the ground and sniffed. He wasn't sure if he could exactly place this particular smell of dirt and so he took out a tiny shovel that he carried in his pocket and dug into the ground. He got a good chunk of damp soil and put it into a small plastic bag. Then he went inside. In a set of drawers that he had bought at an auction for three hundred dollars were dozens of small Tupperware containers. He took out an empty one and shoveled the dirt inside. He labeled the front. September the first. Twenty-one thirty. Front lawn. Slightly earthy. Comforting smell. Probably good before bed for curing nightmares. He picked out a blue container and took off the lid. This sample was from deep in the valley right by the Red Deer River. The soil had a thick, humic odour. He had seen in the museum that the deposits from that part of the badlands were sixty-six million years old. The place used to be a forest. It used to be a jungle buried under an ocean below a swamp so deep in the past that it was almost impossible to believe that he had any connection to it. He smelled the dirt again and then he realized that some of the pieces of dirt that were in those ancient swamps were in him now. His fingers twitched.

Gartner wondered if it were possible to smell age in everything. He ran his fingers over the drawers. The cabinet had been built in 1850, in Brixton, and had been brought over by some of the original settlers. The piece had been in the valley since 1900. Three hundred dollars was a lot to pay for a cabinet that he didn't keep anything in but dirt, but somehow the history attracted him. He put his nose to the wood. There was only a slight smell of varnish and of carved oak. Perhaps it wasn't old enough.

The phone rang. He knew who it would be.

"Hello this place," his dad said. His dad said that every single time he phoned. Gartner laughed and tried to sound happy.

"How's business?" his dad asked.

"We're up a bit." That wasn't strictly true. In fact, they were selling as per normal, but there wasn't anything a bit of creative accounting couldn't fix.

"I guess Denise is going on Friday," his dad said.

"She thinks the earth is going to be taken over by insects."

"She'd know."

There was a long pause on the phone. "Are you going to need any help when she's gone?"

"I don't think so. Business to the museum drops right off after Labour Day. You can come in and help if you want. I'd always like to see you."

"It's your show. How are you feeling these days?"

"I'm feeling fine," he said. Again, not exactly true, but you can't actually tell your father that you're feeling bad. It would just make him feel bad, which would make his mother feel bad, which would make him feel worse.

"Rundle phoned," his dad said.

"Ah, what did he say?"

"He says he'll give me a pretty decent price."

"He wants to turn it into a disco or something, doesn't he?"

"No, he just wants to pump gas. He says he's got some ideas to increase the cash flow."

"Gorgosaurus gasoline, no doubt."

"Something like that."

"Let me think about it for a while," Gartner said. "I know you want to keep the business with us, but it would be a lot of money for you."

"What would you do?"

"I'll be okay."

After his father hung up he could still hear his voice. He went back to the chest of drawers and stared at the Tupperware containers. He opened one up and figured maybe he should re-label the specimen more precisely. Something splashed onto the dirt. Gartner thought maybe it was raining inside his house, but he knew, of course, it couldn't be raining inside the house.

ON SUNDAY MORNING he went to the museum. He wasn't much interested in seeing the huge skeletons anymore. They were good enough, but he'd already seen them a hundred times. He went through the ancient reef section and past the Permian Sea until he came to a long display of tracks. Somewhere, a long time ago, an animal had wandered across a beach. Then, a bird flew in and loitered for a while. Maybe to look for food. Maybe just to walk in the sand. Who knows, birds did those kind of things. Gartner sat down on the bench and stared at the slab of sandstone and petrified tracks. After he watched for a while, he was sure new tracks were being added. Reptile tracks and the swash of a tail on the ground. A dozen more birds lighting, spreading a maze of web and claw imprints onto the ground until the beach looked like an abstract painting. It was as if he was watching a moving picture. He was just going to get up and smell the block when he felt someone beside him. Patty was staring at him. "Hi," he said. She didn't move. Maybe she was staring right past him. He stood up and turned around to see what she was looking at. There wasn't anything there, just a display of plants that had lived during the Devonian period.

"Hi," he said again.

She shook her head. "Oh, Gartner, hi. How are you?"

"I'm good. How are you?"

"I heard you may be selling the gas station."

Not this, Gartner thought. This was absolutely the last thing he wanted to talk about. "Maybe. I'm still thinking about it." He turned and pointed to the sandstone slab. "Amazing, isn't it?"

"Yeah, I guess," she said. "What'll you do if you leave the gas station?"

He shrugged. "I mean, that birds were walking on this dirt millions of years ago and although they're gone these tracks are still here. We can actually see where they were walking."

"Busy day at the beach," she said. "Do you think it's some kind of code?"

"Code?"

"Code. Do you think they were trying to, you know, communicate something?"

"I don't know." Code, like logarithms or the bobbing thing that cuckoo kept on doing? "Do you know that part of the atoms that were in those birds are actually in us today?"

"Oh, gross. You're kidding me."

"That's how small atoms are."

"Don't they die or something after a while?"

Die? Good question, he thought. He had no idea what the life expectancy of an atom was. "I don't know how long they live for."

"How long do you think you'll stay at the station?" Her lip twitched once.

He waved the idea off. "I've still got time to think about it."

"What will you do?"

"Do?"

"Where will you go?"

Gartner was distracted. Something on Patty smelled very old, like dust. Like dust on an unpaved road late in the summer just about sunset.

"What's that smell?" he asked.

"What smell?"

"That smell on you."

Patty's eyes opened up and her shoulder drew away from Gartner. Her brow knitted. "I don't smell."

"No, I mean, it smells like earth. Is it cologne?"

"I'm not wearing any."

Brilliant, Gartner thought.

"But um, codes," he said. "Yeah, they could be codes. I mean something from a long time ago could be trying to communicate with us in weird ways."

"Maybe it's my shampoo."

"Shampoo. Yeah, it smells, like, old."

"Great."

"Nostalgic," he said.

"Yeah, weird communication," she said. "Yeah. Sure. I think you're right on that one."

"I didn't mean it smelled bad like dirt or anything. Smells can be nostalgic in a good way."

"Dirt?"

"Or, well, even shampoo."

"Oh sure, I guess. But it's coded. I mean it could be coded."

"Definitely coded."

"The gas station has smells."

"Never thought of it that way. The bakery has, too. Bread, flowers."

"How long are you staying for, actually?"

"I don't know."

"Well, I'll bring you some flowers before you go."

Gartner reached inside his pocket and fished around.

"I've got something for you," he said.

"You've got something for me?"

"Absolutely." Gartner went through a frenzy of pocket searching. Finally from his vest coat pocket he pulled out a small bottle that had been carefully wrapped in tissue paper. She opened it.

"Gartner, it's plant fertilizer."

"I noticed that a few of your plants and a couple of your cacti in the window were looking sick. Probably the soil. Starved for nutrients, so I thought I'd pick it up for you."

He realized in the minute of silence, he had not breathed, she had not spoken.

"Well, that's kind of weird," she said, finally.

Weird? he thought.

"But if they do any better with this, I'll make sure I bring some blooms by the gas station."

He wondered why she kept bringing up the gas station.

THE PRAIRIE TALKS without being lonely, Gartner thought. Not like people. The snow melts in the spring. The grain comes up in the summer. Everything connects. Wherever the prairie is going, it always arrives on time. He went through the morning rituals of setting out the signs, shelving the oil, and running out the air hoses.

Rundle came around the corner. He had an old bright red Chev that he'd fixed up. When he turned off the road into the lot, the fin of his car brushed the metal sign that read Regular Gas 49 cents a litre. Rundle pulled up beside the pump and shut his engine off.

"You should move that sign out of the way," he said. He wore a cowboy hat. There was something about hats Gartner didn't like. Maybe he didn't like any kind of hat, but he wasn't sure.

"Why?"

"Because someone's going to run it over and then you'd have a lawsuit on your hands. People go to court over everything these days. Can you imagine the psychological trauma suffered by some-one who runs into a sign like that?"

"You want some gas?"

"Fill 'er up."

Gartner took off the cap to the Chev and stuck the nozzle in. Rundle leaned back on the hood and stared up to the azure sky like the autumn was his to own. "I was talking to your dad yester-day."

"I'm sure you were. What did he say?"

"He said he wasn't sure if you were going to stay or he was going to sell it. He also said something strange about insects inheriting the earth."

"Ah, well, here's the reason." Gartner turned his head towards Denise who was making her way across the lot.

"This is a 1956, isn't it?" She was eating a croissant.

"That's right." Rundle seemed surprised.

"But it's got a 302 in it now." She spread peanut butter over the croissant.

"Smart gal."

Denise walked around the car and motioned at the hood. Rundle nodded. She undid the latch and gave long looks of approval as she stuffed the last of the roll into her mouth.

"Do you want to go for a ride?" Rundle asked.

"Absolutely," she said and then looked at Gartner.

"Hell, drive it as far as Saskatchewan."

Rundle opened the passenger door, but Denise went around to the driver's side.

"Where did you get that roll?" Gartner asked.

"At the bakery," she said, and put the car into gear. "But you can't get them anymore. She's closed up for the day. Gone some-where."

"Gone?" Gartner asked. "Where?"

"No clue. Said she had to fill some deficits."

"Deficits?"

"Women always talk in codes," Rundle said.

Denise hit the gas and the Chev flew out of the parking lot. Rundle got bounced against the headrest then tried to get his seatbelt on.

Gartner turned around and went inside. He sat at his desk and watched the bird bob up and down. He got up and pulled the bird out of the water and broke its neck in half. Then he ripped the head off and crushed the beak beneath his boot. After that, he yarded the little pink feet off the legs, broke its wings in two, and threw them out the door.

HE GOT HIS shovel and a dozen plastic bags. Where the sign had read Back at 5:00, he crossed out five o'clock with a crayon and wrote in tomorrow. Then he walked out into the Badlands. The gullies rose on all sides of him in white stratified layers. Most of the cacti had finished flowering, but there was still the smell in the air of sage and something just about ready to open into a bright blossom. He took his shovel and got down on his knees. He took a handful of earth and pressed it into his face. He could imagine the years of grass and shrub that had grown and died, broken down the rock to form the dirt. He saw the railway being laid. He saw bands of ancients settling along the river. He saw buffalo.

And then he saw a tiny gas station sitting on the corner of the road with a man looking glumly out at traffic. Regular 49 cents a litre. He pictured a man, even older than his father, dying, being buried and turning back into dirt. The water from his eyes slipped down between his fingers and then he saw a flat piece of stone, no bigger than a quarter was stuck on his palm. There was a delicate pattern imprinted on the face. Tiny, but undeniably a set of petrified wings. Maybe of a fly or a grasshopper. The lattice was perfect. Two wings, no head, no body, just wings. The odour off the rock struck Gartner in the middle of his temple. Primordial, humic, like life from very far back. He licked the stone to taste the age, as if by being close to the wings he might suddenly take to the air. He got up. He felt dizzy. He stared up at the white September sun and could not see a shadow anywhere and then a figure in the gulley moved. On the other side of the gulley Patty also stood up. She had cacti in her hand. Her cheeks were dirty. She was fifty yards away, but there was no mistaking her. She looked right at him and then turned away. She walked out of the gulley and into the aspen grove too casually to be believed.

"WHAT HAPPENED?" Denise asked when he got back to the station. "I hate to be the one to tell you this, but you look like shit."

"I feel like shit," he said.

"Why?" she said.

"I was out in the Badlands sniffing dirt and the woman from the bakery saw me."

"That's pretty bad."

Gartner got old in the ring and put his hand on the register. He stared at his face in a mirror that the bank had supplied free of charge two decades ago. He was truly covered with dirt. Not the sweated dirt from a man you'd seen working on a farm all day or someone doing roadwork making the highways safe to drive, but the kind of dirt you'd expect to see on a disheveled drunk rolling in the ditch where all his friends could see him crying into the storm sewer.

"You smashed up the cuckoo," Denise said.

"I hate that bird."

"You'd watch it for hours."

"I hate the smell of gasoline. I hate the smell of oil. I hate this corner. I hate what I'm doing to my father and I hate mirrors from banks."

"But you like the smell of dirt."

"I like the smell of dirt."

"Dirt turns into oil." She pulled off her baseball cap, sat down at the desk and thumbed through a brochure on air filters.

"I know that."

"Nothing wrong with collecting dirt. Hell, I do it all the time."

"No you don't."

"Okay. I don't. But what I'm saying is we all do some pretty strange things and it's no big deal. I mean, are you that concerned Patty saw your dirty face or that she saw you shoveling dirt into little bags to take home and sniff?"

"I don't do that."

Denise picked up a blue Tupperware container with a label that read 'Horseshoe Canyon light brown. Nostalgic. Fertile aroma.' "It's okay, really. I mean, it doesn't bother me. It's not like you're smelling girls' underwear or something." She paused. "You don't do that, do you, Gart?"

"Only if they were soiled," he said, and thought it was pretty funny, but Denise didn't laugh.

A BLUE DODGE wheeled around the corner and took out the metal sign at the corner of the lot. There was the sound of a hard edge scraping against a car door and the truculent swearing of an unhappy driver.

Gartner figured that if he had been going slower, he ought to have seen the sign swinging in the wind, but he decided to push it out of the way anyhow. He dragged the battered post towards the fence. When he looked down, he saw a cactus growing in a crack of the pavement. A bright blue flower blossomed on the top of the leaf.

"Are you going to get me some gas?" the driver said.

"Only if you slow down."

"Your sign ruined my paint."

"You were driving too fast."

"I'm calling the cops."

"Do it."

GARTNER FILLED THE little tub halfway with soil and then nestled the cactus inside with transplant juice. He put the plant on the inside of the station window where the bird used to be. The more he sniffed at it, the more restless he got.

"Just do it, for crying out loud," Denise said.

Gartner took the plant, walked out of the station, and down the street towards town. Everywhere rose the smell of harvest in the soil, of the past being churned up into the light of the present. He wondered if anyone else could smell the excitement except for him. In a few moments, he stood at the door of the bakery and his fingers twitched around the pot. Maybe Denise would call the police. Perhaps she would laugh at him. The room was filled with the smell of sugar and flour. Gartner endured a brief image of dirt turning into grain and then into bread and then sitting on the shelf in front of him as a loaf.

"Gartner?" Patty said and came out of the back room. She was covered in flour and had on white coveralls.

"I brought you this flower," he said. "I'd seen that you'd had a couple in the window, but not a blue one."

She wiped off her hands and came around the counter. "I've been looking for a blue flower for months. They have a name, but I can't remember what it is."

Gartner felt a wave of relief wash over him and she put it in the window. She turned around and smiled at him. She was wearing a bakery hat, but Gartner didn't mind.

IN EACH OUR
CELLAR

I HAD WANTED to be a hit man. Or an astrophysicist or perhaps
a neurosurgeon or at least an elite csis agent. But instead, I
became a paleontologist. Not even a paleontologist, really, but a
Sediment Assistant, which meant I threw buckets of dirt through
a sieve and looked for near microscopic bone chips. Pretty bor-
ing. Anyone could have done it and at minimum wage not many
people did. The mosquitoes were fierce and the cattle in the Red
Deer valley had a strange bowel disease so their feces smelled
like fennel. You got a certificate at the end of August. Basically,
this was the worst summer of my life.

The Tyrell didn't pay for accommodation, but on the rear wall
of the field lab there was a chalkboard where museum friendly
houses were posted. That meant cheap. The house I picked up
was a curved aluminum shed on the banks of the river inhabited
by three ancient hippies and a redneck rancher named Barb who
categorized their Quonset as a homestead. (Note: Barb, a perver-
sion of the Icelandic Bjartpor Brynjolfsson, was a guy . . . not like
the Barbie and Ken dolls, and hated being referred to as such.)

Barb owned the greatest amount of pot imaginable to mankind. The weed was bound up in square bales and stored in a hidden cavern beneath the kitchen floor. He doled his dope out in return for bizarre social covenants and a promise that we would never call Immigration on him. Barb wove this narrative about how he grew the stuff in Panama to give to the poor, but when the Americans invaded he was forced to fly the weed out of the Canal Zone to Alberta where he settled to fight injustice and Fascism in the early nineties. None of us believed him. The weed was of terrible quality and smelled of peat moss. There was just a lot of it. Probably Barb had nursed the tea pitifully in a BC greenhouse then brought it with him so he could make friends easier. Besides his pot, he didn't have a lot of admirable qualities. Barb was violent and unpredictable. He cussed, was prone to bouts of paranoia and often stalked the veranda of the Quonset wearing nothing but a Stetson and leather belt while he made up stories about his adventures in the Vietnam War.

Also on the farm were Dingle and his wife, Evita, who both left Vancouver for the Badlands in the mid-nineties. Then there was Tinny, a lithesome redhead who spent her days doing crossword puzzles and flaunting her front end. Tinny had no interest whatsoever in anything sexual, or at least not with me. The four of them spent their summer days living on the rundown farm, drinking Canadian Club, and smoking weed. Nobody worked. Everyone made ceramic pots. About twice a week one of them went completely psycho and threatened some melodramatic form of self-harm.

That's where I came in. Through my paleontogical connections I had befriended a young lad by the name of Edmund who delivered pharmaceuticals for a local drugstore. Edmund had an unhealthy fixation with the extinct Cretaceous bird Pteranodon. He was convinced a clutch of the creatures lived somewhere in the Badlands and were intent on hunting him down for a food source. Of course Edmund was mental and had no friends. He hung around the excavation pit looking for tidbits of information on Pteranodon safety, or sympathetic conversation. I tolerated him, let him sort the gravel, and gave him free sandwiches supplied by the museum. Sometimes I think I exploited his labour. There was no chance whatsoever we would ever find any Pteranodon bones in the sieves, but I didn't tell Edmund that. In return for my affections, Edmund would supply me with bottles of Oxazepam that somehow went missing from the monthly drugstore inventory. Sometimes two or three at a time. Barb and Dingle needed downers. I needed a place to stay. It was that easy.

On the last Tuesday of August, I pulled into the farm from a totally unproductive day in the fossil pits and heard a number of sharp cracks break through the blue prairie sky. Maybe a thunderstorm, maybe an oil derrick exploding or the Bleriot Ferry ramming into its mooring docks once again. The pilot was often intoxicated. But nothing on the farm had changed. I was confronted with the usual broken weather vane, dormant kiln, and assortment of cannibalized automobiles. The tractor shed scorched in the sun, a humble coyote lumbered into a ditch. It was thirty-seven degrees celsius in the shade.

Dingle sat in a rocking chair smoking a pipe. His dog was curled up at his feet. Dingle was fifty, had a long face and blonde hair and always seemed to be just waking up. The bowl of his pipe was embossed with a likeness of Leon Trotsky.

"Barb is freaking out," he said.

"Why this time?"

"God knows. Too much weed, I guess. He tried to clean his ear out with an electric drill and now there's blood all over the Quonset."

"Is he hurt?" I said.

"Probably."

"Where is he now?"

"Had to lock him in the shed," Dingle said. "Not sure if that was a good idea or not. There's plenty of tools in there he could hurt himself with that don't need power."

"I could give him a downer."

"Please."

I sat down on the chair next to Dingle and patted the dog. The smelly old creature basically liked the world but was flatulent on account of the black bean diet that Tinny kept him on. At that moment Tinny stepped out onto the porch in her thin veneer of a cotton shirt. She must have known I was thinking about her.

"Are you two men going to do anything about this situation?" she said.

"I could run into town and get some beer," Dingle said.

"Look, he's your friend."

"Someone has to get beer."

"Hang on," I said. "I'll go and talk to him. Back me up, all right, Tinny. Maybe we can get the Yin and Yang female persuasion thing going."

In truth, I didn't think Tinny's presence would help one bit. She had a bad habit of coming up with onerous Susan Sontag lines whenever men pissed her off by emulating Hemingway, but facing Barb alone meant enduring an endless lecture on the Fourteenth Amendment. We walked across our dustbin of a back yard. There's a thin line between awesome and ugly and we were there. Prickly pear cacti, broken stubby beer bottles, and rusted parts from diesel engines that could have been sixty years old, made the ground lunar.

"Take a couple of those pots into town for me," Tinny said.

"Why?"

"Money. Canadian Tire will pay two bucks each for them. It's a rip off, though. They turn around and sell them as Mexican imports for fifteen."

The shed was a huge corrugated iron box big enough to fit a pickup truck into. The walls were hot to touch. Just the kind of place that Nazis would have put POWs into when they were bad. The door was bolted shut from the inside.

"Go away," Barb said.

"It's a hundred and fifty degrees in there," I said. "You'll die of dehydration."

"So be it. I am master of my own fate."

"Goddammit," Tinny said and kicked the door. "Open the lock, you moron."

"No way."

"Why?"

"You wouldn't believe me if I told you."

"You're right," Tinny said. "I wouldn't. Open the door."

"Barb, I'm listening," I said.

"It's Manifest Destiny," Barb said. "The Yanks are coming to get me. I told you bastards you shouldn't have voted Conservative."

"I've got some downers. Open the door and I'll give you a couple."

There was a long silence inside the shed. Then Barb sniffled. "Pinks or yellows?"

"Pinks."

Maybe a minute passed, maybe two, then the deadbolt slipped aside and the base of the door creaked half a note.

"Yeah, yeah," he said.

I pushed the handle open and stepped inside. The stifling dark smelled of sawdust and motor oil heavier than life itself. Barb stood naked in the corner behind an air compressor. His skin was covered in sweat and dried blood ran in branches from his ear to his shoulder.

"Put them on the work bench," he said. "But first, we share a joint."

"That's not what we need right now."

"It's what I need. We've got to go to the fifth level."

"What's the fifth level?"

"Just do it," Tinny said from the other side of the doorway. "Get this over with. There's deer flies out here."

Getting stoned at four in the afternoon was not something I wanted to do. The summer heat and Tinny's heaving bow would leave me in a state of unbearable frustration from which there would be no recovery. Perhaps I could fake a few tokes, slip him the downers and go swimming in the river.

"All right," I said. "Stay cool and we'll get this fixed. Think calm blue ocean."

"I hate the water," he said.

"Gently rustling wheat and cold beer then."

"Okay," he said. "Tinny too. This has to be like a group prayer session."

Tinny stuck her head in the door but then recoiled. "Jesus," she said. "Put some pants on at least."

"It's damn hot in here," he said, but by then Tinny had retreated to the far side of the potato patch where she readjusted her sandals.

Barb produced a sweat-drenched joint from behind his bloodied ear and in a moment the shed was filled with green smoke. Then he swallowed the two pinks and washed them down with some flat ginger ale.

"Well?" I said.

"They're coming for me, man. They've got my number. The outside of the shed is riddled with bullets."

"Tinny said you tried to drill your eardrum out with a home appliance."

"She's being melodramatic."

"Can you still hear?"

"Of course I can still hear," he said. "There are bullet holes all over the place. I was drilling one of the pots and the rounds raked through the window."

Yep, sure enough the window was smashed. A coffee pot on the work bench had been completely perforated too. I ran my finger over the riddled oak.

"Probably bird shot."

"Take a closer look, Sherlock."

Okay, definitely not buckshot. Or a .22. The issue was more the sheer number of rounds than the calibre; there must have been a dozen slugs in the wall.

"Maybe hunters," I suggested. They were always drunk and hunting out of season in this part of the world.

"Or maybe Special Ops posing as hunters. Look at that group-ing. That's expertise."

"Barb, you owe taxes in the US. Nothing more."

Maybe Barb's stomach was empty, maybe the heat had speeded up his metabolism, or maybe he just wanted to be loved, but in a few moments his face slackened and he sighed. Dingle's Chev rambled down the driveway from town.

"Dingle's got beer," I said. "Come on, man. We'll tape up your ear and sort this out later."

"Fricken CIA," Barb said and picked up his jeans off the dirt floor.

Outside, the harsh Badland sun was blinding and all the dead dinosaurs from beneath the earth rose up to make me nervous. I had ingested too much ganga in the shed. The gunshots had shaken me up. The valley bottom became a cruel angular place with threats hidden behind every grain silo. I watched Tinny rearrange her chassis again as she talked on her cellphone, and the cosmos clicked one second closer to panic attack.

Barb, on the other hand, was doing much, much better. He stuffed an oil rag into his ear and rubbed some bitter bush under his cheeks like it was aftershave. Then he strode across the dead corn garden to Dingle's truck and opened up the beer cooler.

"One cold Canadian there my fellow countryman," he said. "God, you guys build good beer and good rivers and good hockey games. When's the game on, anyway?"

"Uh, two months?" Dingle said and popped open a brownie on the bumper of his Chev. Barb snatched the prize up, downed it in one swallow, then found another.

"I barely escaped assassination, you know."

"Really?"

"Someone put a fair few rounds through the shed," I said.

We went inside the house. Barb sat down at the table and flicked on the remote channel changer looking for a hockey game. He liked sitting at the table when he watched TV. One of his secret hatches that went down to the stash was hidden beneath the floorboards and he knew he could access it any time in case a commercial came on he didn't like.

Evita came in, set some ceramic pots on the table, and seemed concerned about my welfare. "You look pale," she said.

Barb had found a hockey game. Finland versus Czechoslovakia, but that didn't matter to him. He was happy. Then from down the road came a whirlwind of dust and I suspected the worst; a great anger from Hades had erupted through the torrid earth and was about to consume all of us alive.

"What's that?" Dingle said.

"Is it a tornado?"

"No," Evita said. "I think it's a car."

"Are we expecting someone?"

"The cops," Tinny said. She stepped in the back door and stuffed her cellphone down a sweat-soaked shirt pocket. "I called the cops."

"You what?" Barb said.

"I heard what you said in the shed, Barb. And for once, I believed you. If there's a bunch of right-wing ranchers taking pot shots at us, the police have to know. We could get hurt."

"Are you nucking futs?" Barb said and jumped out of the chair while pulling on a large clump of scalp.

"No, I am the only sane one around here. The last thing we need is a bunch of vigilante revenge killings starting between you and the neighbours."

"You're standing on enough weed to have us imprisoned for the rest of eternity."

"They don't care about that stuff anymore."

Barb went to the window. The patrol car had stopped outside the house and the dust was still coming. "I'm going to be execut- ed in Guantanamo Bay."

"I think that may be a bit rash," Dingle said.

"Go down into the basement and secure the weed," Barb said to me. "Pull the cellophane tarp over the bale and then turn the air scrubber on and wind up the zippers. I'll try and stall this dick until we get things under control."

Barb took a huge tablecloth from the cupboard and threw it over the kitchen table. The edges draped down to the floor concealing the hatch from sight. By this time, I figured the dice of doom were pretty much cast and it was too hot to run anywhere, so I headed for the bathroom where Barb had drilled emergency super-secret trap door number two beneath the sink. Just as I turned the handle, Tinny opened the front door and the good constable stepped up onto the ledge. Blonde, freckles. Maybe it was her armoured vest, or maybe it was the weed distorting my hormonal sense of perspective, but at once I loved her and only her and there was going to be no controlling the horrible state of desire that then possessed me and my common sense.

"May I come in?" she said.

"Please," Tinny said.

"I was close by and figuring on the nature of your call, I figured I'd stop by right away."

"Thank you. We were quite frightened."

"No we weren't," Barb said.

"Shut up, Barb," Tinny said.

"Is anyone hurt?"

"We're fine, constable," Barb said. "Please go away."

"He smokes far too much weed, constable," Tinny said. "All these men do and they're incapable of making rational decisions when it comes to public safety."

"I hope no one is irrational right now."

"No ma'am," Barb said and then to me: "Ognay ownstairsdnay."

I was unable to formulate anything witty to add to the conversation anyway. Something in my underwear snarled into a triangle and then inverted itself into a starfish and there was a fifty percent chance I had drool on my lip. Slipping into the bathroom I locked the door behind me and deftly lifted up the false bottom of the floor beneath the sink. Barb's underground cellar was exactly what you'd think any underground cellar belonging to a paranoid, dope smoking para-revolutionary would look like. Rows of tinned beans lined the wall, machetes and Picasso look-alikes settled into the dirt. This was the place the survivor artiste would outlive the apocalypse. The ceiling was encrusted with a tangle of copper wire and plumbing fixtures, and a deep sense of claustrophobia clouded the air. In the far corner of the basement, beneath a yellow caged light, sat my target: four rotten bales of stalky brown ganga and they must have weighed ten pounds each. I was in the middle of zippering up the top bale when the strobe of light struck me from above. Barb had cut spy holes into the floor that were angled so the spy could see up but no one could see down. Then there was the creaking of heavy boots, people talking and laughing, and Finland scored. The chairs scraped and I realized that Barb, Dingle, Tinny, and the visiting constable were all sitting at the kitchen table directly above my head watching the game.

"Isn't this old?" the constable said.

"Oh no," Barb said. "It's only about to happen."

"Pardon?"

"See what I mean?" Tinny said.

"There are some dubious odours up and about," the good constable said.

"We've had a rash of skunks in the valley," Barb said. "They walk right into the house and make their nests beneath the floorboards like they own the place."

"Even the young ones smell," Dingle said.

I stood up on a stool and peered through one of the spy holes. I could see the checkered tablecloth, the chair, and the yellow stripe on the constable's trouser. She crossed her legs and a strip of tanned flesh exposed itself above the top of her boot. Her skin was a carmine deeper than the broken beer bottles in our field or the layers of silt that washed into the playa. And when she reached down under the tablecloth to scratch her tender limb, I saw it—the tattoo of a red cherub set to strike its victim with a golden arrow—and knew what had to be done. There was no turning back, there never had been and couldn't be now. Centimetre at a time I pushed up on the wooden hatch. The stealth of my movements amazed even me. Part mongoose, part seducer, my jaw crept forward along the floorboards and my mouth opened wide. Just as my tongue closed the last inch to her delicate flesh I reflected on what love might taste like and how for centuries the Red Deer River had cut into the earth, down into the hearts of the lonely and wore away the pain from the sad.

ANYTHING MORE PERFECT

A PIECE OF fescue wilted over a hubcap, and if there were a more perfect summer moment in the trailer park, Edward did not know it. The baking asphalt, stagnant dryer lint, and maturing crankcase oil all told him summer would stay through the end of September, perhaps through the end of time, and that was a virtuous tenure. For September was by far the best weather for suntanning, weed smoking, beer drinking, porn watching and really the best weather for everything in life, including just sitting beside the drained swimming pool and watching the middle-aged cougars go brown before the first frost crept onto the diving board.

Sometimes the perfection was so intense Edward heard radio static cackling out of nowhere or bison bones snapping in the dry grass. That last one scared him, as if he were being watched by his girlfriend, or the police. Maybe even by an ancient animal that lived somewhere in the trailer court and knew when he was peeking through the neighbour's window, lifting a quart of wine, or rolling up a slim of skunkweed.

He readjusted the bag of bud in his pocket so it was concealed from whomever might be watching, and walked across the trout bridge to the swimming pool. Mrs. Seltzer's deck chair was there, as were her sunglasses, her vodka tonic, and romance novel, but there was no browning Mrs. Seltzer. He listened for the squeal of Mr. Davidson's shortwave box, but that was gone too, and so finally at lot twenty-nine he stopped and stared at a bleached garden elf who poked a shovel into a pit of petunias.

Shea stepped out onto the porch and emptied her ashtray into the still air. "Did you get it?"

"I got it."

The screen door crashed behind them. A commercial was on the television about children starving in Ethiopia.

"Where did it come from?"

"The West Coast."

"So it's hydroponic?"

"It's not."

"I hate hydroponic." She lit up a Player's Light. A Mixmaster was going in the kitchen. "It's got all kinds of chemicals on it."

"This hasn't."

"How do you know that?"

"The guy told me."

"What guy?"

"The guy from Salt Spring Island."

"He's an idiot."

"When he moves out here and starts his own greenhouse then you won't be saying that."

"It's thirty below here in January."

"He'll use convective lenses."

"It's probably been sprayed with Agent Orange," she said.

Shea snapped her slippers against her heel. Edward liked her feet but not the slippers. The heat made the trailer groan. He was afraid one day the house would slide into the Red Deer River. An improvised seismometer made out of tuning forks and piano wire trembled on the fridge. The machine ran on AA batteries and sometimes went off before electric storms. He reset the dial with a spoon.

"That thing doesn't work," she said.

"It does."

"It didn't go off when the house just moved."

"That's because it moved from the heat. Not an earthquake. It knows the difference."

"Did you get beer?"

"What did you want to do?"

"Get loaded," she said. "Watch a movie."

"Which one?"

"How about that one where that guy does that stuff?"

Edward sat down on the couch and picked up a copy of *Toro-Saurus* magazine. This was the last one before it went out of print so he was hoping the issue would become a collector's item. On page nine a woman slicked down with Lycra-lizard cream toked on a porcelain hookah. Edward felt a rumble move up the leg of the sofa.

"Do you want to go out to the club tonight?" he said.

"No."

"Why not?"

"We went last week."

The fleeting odour of Brazilian nuts twisted in the air and Edward thought he heard people arguing through the wall.

"Why are the radio and TV on at the same time?" he said.

"The radio isn't on."

"I can hear it."

"It's not on."

Edward walked to the bedroom door. The frame stuck on account of the sagged foundation. The radio was off. He sat back down on the couch and replaced the batteries in the seismometer. "Why don't we have what's her face and Jackson over?"

"Chantal and Jackson?

"Yeah, them."

Chantal could be a bitch, but Jackson meant more beer, weed, loud stereo music, and then decent pornography.

"They're pigs."

"Pigs? What do you mean, pigs?"

"They're swingers, Ed."

"So what?"

"You want to suck his dick or what?"

"No."

"Why don't you just admit it?"

"I don't."

The radio static shot up again and then a flock of magpies screamed across the roof. Edward stalked back into the bedroom. He pulled the radio off the nightstand and threw it against the wall. One of the dials rolled under the dresser.

"What are you doing?" Shea said.

"That radio was driving me crazy."

"Quit freaking out."

"I'm not freaking out."

"Look, go ahead, have them over," she said. "I don't care. I'm just saying I don't want to get into any weird stuff with them."

"You're the one who drank the Slippery Eel out of her navel."

"That's different." She picked up a copy of *Chatelaine*. "We're girls. I was drunk."

"How about I give Davidson a call."

Shea gave him the look over the top of her magazine. "He's weird too. Besides, you two just get pissed and go on about the Fenian Raids, then you go looking for fossils all night and what fun is that for me? You never find anything anyway."

"I give up. What do you want to do?"

"I can't stay up late," she said. "I'm getting up early in the morning."

"Why?"

"I'm taking an interior designing course."

Edward stared around the room. There was a pink couch circa 1979, some red shag carpet from when Jimi Hendrix was alive, and a bullfighting picture on the wall that predated imagination.

"In the name of all things that are holy, why?"

"Because I have a flair and I can make millions."

"This entire municipality isn't worth a million dollars."

"That's exactly why we'll have to go somewhere else."

A black-and-orange caterpillar made its way up the door frame right in front of his face in the stifling heat. The creature reared its head as if it had something profound to say, but then didn't bother and slithered away.

"We'll have to go wherever the market is," she said.

"You've never shown any interest in interior design."

She picked up a glass of gin and tonic in one motion while keeping her index finger extended. It shook a little. She had been rehearsing this one. "You just haven't noticed. You haven't noticed anything I've done. All you're interested in is this stupid valley and its sordid sex parties. Well, I have talent. I have plans."

She walked over to the window but took a step too close and her nose struck the glass. An ice cube bounced off the floor.

"You're loaded," he said.

"Not near as loaded as you'll be tonight."

"You have to have, like, math and physics and architecture courses for that."

"Why do you keep bringing that up? Every time I want to do something, it's always my education you bring up."

"I'm just saying, what's wrong with the way things are?"

"Let me see. What's wrong with spending the rest of my life working in an Econo Lodge and pandering to arrogant tourists? What's wrong with living in a trailer park that stinks of coagulating Chinese food until the next ice age comes? What's wrong with pre-death cryogenics? Let me think some more."

Pandering was trouble. Coagulating was trouble. Cryogenics even worse. Whenever Shea threw in big words, that was trouble.

"It's not that bad," he said.

"It is that bad. I'm done. I'm not living in a dust bowl. I don't like collecting Dogwood moths or talking about string theory and I'm not hanging around with a bunch of freaks who hump fossils."

"The trailer is on a historic site from the First World War."

"Shut up."

Edward went to the fridge, pulled out a beer, and then picked up her package of Player's Lights.

"Don't turn away from me when I'm talking to you," she said.

"You've finished."

"Bring back my cigarettes."

He put his fingers on the screen door and the latch broke off.

One of the springs exploded across the veranda, got caught it an updraft, and made its way to freedom.

"Where are you going with my cigarettes?" she said.

"Over to screw Mrs. Seltzer."

A sharp pain cut across the back of his skull. Shea's ashtray bounced against the transom and shattered. There was blood and shards of brown glass in his hair and she threw the magazine, the channel changer, and a vase as well.

"Go screw her then."

Her face was ugly and contorted and Edward figured he'd do just that. He went down the wooden stairs, across the children's park with its dried milkweed and rusted teeter-totters, and towards the empty swimming pool.

Still no Mrs. Seltzer, but in the bottom of the pool there was a layer of orange poplar leaves. Flat and thin they spread across the tiles like carpet. Edward picked up a tube of her suntan oil and spread it out over his hand. It smelled of palm and pineapples and he imagined her on a tropical beach, Hawaii maybe, Costa Rica probably, rubbing her neck and chest and then lying back on her deck chair moistly bronzed. The next moment, Edward found himself walking through a thorn bush trellis and down the gravel road towards her trailer at number twenty-seven. He'd extol the social virtues of the romance novel as an opening line.

Number twenty-seven was the most archaic lot in the court. Narrow and grey, the paint peeled off the weathered siding and the windows were translucent with dust. A dozen birdcages hung empty from the rafters and dried paint pots were lined up to the door as if waiting to use the washroom. He had never seen her paint, nor her husband ever be present, and wondered why he even referred to her as Mrs. Seltzer.

The door was half open and Edward stood with his fist poised against the wood. Purple shag on the floor, a pink couch with a spring poking through the fabric, a velvet painting of a Navajo woman riding a lion. Gin bottles, bongs, and a curious tangle of aluminum chopsticks that looked as if they would pick up FM frequencies were scattered across the carpet.

He stepped in, picked the contraption up and one of the sticks caught on a pair of red panties. He ran the underwear between his fingertips. He smelled the inside. He pushed his tongue over the elastic band and the fabric was so coarse, so tarnished and ion charged, he stuffed as much of it as he could inside his mouth and the dried grass all around the trailer fractured and snapped in excitement.

From down the hall came a tiny gasp. Edward threw the panties under the couch. He couldn't recall if he was supposed to be an insurance salesman or the trailer park inspector or just a Good Samaritan who had heard a woman cry for help. When a second gasp came, this time lower and longer, Edward waited to hear if a male grunt followed suit. But there was none. Only a woman's sinuous moan coming from the toilet and he could not recall if his CPR certificate was valid. He imagined leaning over the tanned Mrs. Seltzer and pumping the life-giving air back into her body that would make her forever grateful and Shea forever contrite.

He went down the hall, pushed open the bathroom door, and was soaked in light and steam. The roof had been replaced with a plastic dome. The gorgeous September sun heated the room to jungle proportions. Amazon green and begonia pink. Through the curls of moisture, the nude and tanned Mrs. Seltzer stood squeezed upright in the shower with her breasts pressed against the glass. A tide of honey liquid flooded up over her arms and shoulders while she remained sealed in her huge test tube. The oil poured from a faucet at the top of the shower and smelled of all things tropical. For a moment their eyes locked and then Mrs. Seltzer's lips parted and she looked heavenward and Edward saw it too: an entire oil drum of the fluid poised to drown the frenzied act. A siphon hose curled down from the roof into the shower capsule that had been sealed shut with putty. Sealed shut from the inside.

Edward's mouth dried out. His genitals snarled in his pants. He raised one hand towards the flood of caramel around Mrs. Seltzer's face and saw the perfect oval of bliss form in her eyes. A second of panic cracked across her lips as the oil washed inside her nose, but then he was running, running down the hall, out the door, and stealing through the dried pampas grass in the courtyard. He fled past number forty-four where the residents planted tulips patiently every May, and through a tangle of short wave antennae wires that hummed in excitement.

When he got back home, the sun seemed lower. Sitting on the couch and threading the bag of weed through his hands, he wondered how long he had actually spent watching his neighbour in her bathroom. If seconds weren't criminal, hours probably were.

"Are you going to smoke that stuff or what?" Shea said. She came out of the kitchen with her hair done up in a mass of steam curlers. The bottle of gin was half gone.

"What?"

"Where did you go?"

"Tanning," he said and walked over to the table to pick up the channel changer. The frame had been broken in half and the red on-off button smeared with blood which was probably his.

"You don't look any browner."

"What movie did you want to watch?"

"Roll me some of that hydroponic and we'll figure it out."

"Want to watch some porn first?"

"Why would I want to watch porn first?"

"I just thought you might be in the mood."

"You spend half your life sticking your nose into other people's lives and then you come home and expect me to be in the mood and do the dirty work."

Edward used the *Audubon Guide to Prairie Birds* as a rolling board. His knees kept trembling so the bud rattled out between his legs.

"What's wrong with you?" She sat beside him with a fresh gin and tonic.

Outside the sky turned a sunset orange and a velvet striped grasshopper rattled its saber in the bush. At first Edward thought it was a grasshopper, but the whine became louder and more urgent and then the parking lot was filled with red and blue lights that settled at the end of the road.

He stood at the window with his joint and watched the paramedics run to door number twenty-seven. The interior lights of the trailer flicked on one by one.

"Don't stand there with that weed," Shea said. "There's cops there. This isn't Vancouver, you know."

"They're going into Seltzer's place."

"So did you fuck her to death or what?"

"I didn't do that."

"Of course you didn't do that. She's a prime-time cougar and you're thirty pounds overweight."

Edward picked up his pair of Zeiss binoculars. Through the lenses grainy shapes moved around through the trailer and then a collapsible gurney was wheeled towards the bathroom.

"She put on a show for me in her shower," he said.

"You smoke too much weed, Ed," she said. "I really have no clue why I stay with you."

A constable got out of her squad car and began coiling yellow police tape around the trailer using alders as corner posts. Then two paramedics wheeled the gurney out and whatever was on it was wrapped in a plastic green sheet.

Shea let the curlers fall off her shoulder. "Eddy, what the hell are they taking out of there?" She seized the glasses from Edward's hands and the leather neck strap broke. As she adjusted the focus on the lenses, her mouth got angular and ugly again. "You did go in there."

"I told you."

"You idiot."

"It was bondage stuff."

"Where?"

"In her shower."

"You watched her?"

"She wanted me to," Edward said.

Shea threw the binoculars down on the floor. "Why didn't you do something?"

"Like what?"

"Pull her out."

"She was enjoying herself."

"Goddammit Ed, you left her there?"

"Of course I left her there."

"Why?"

"People do their thing."

Shea staggered over and collapsed on the couch. The light from the television screen flickered her face green. She sucked down her last bit of gin then crunched on an ice cube. In the still of the September night the air moved slightly and the smell of desert plants and tanned bodies drifted through the trailer court.

"That's why you stink," she said. "You have her goddamn tanning oil all over you."

"Just on my shoes."

"I can't believe you left that woman there to die."

"She was fine when I left her."

"Get out of my house," she said. She stood up and clenched her fists and they went white and then her cheeks went white and she turned and plucked the bullfighting picture off the wall, and struck him over the head. The velvet snapped and the wood frame split in half.

"It's my house," Edward said.

"Get out."

Edward went out into the night sky. Down the alley the medics slid the gurney into the back of the ambulance and there were red and blue lights exploding like flash bulbs. He tripped over the antenna wire that ran from Davidson's shortwave to an elm tree and a barred owl swooped into the darkness.

"You pig. You asshole." Shea kicked him in the ribs. Then she peeled off her pink slipper and smacked him over the head with the heel. "What kind of man are you, anyway?"

Edward got up, pushed her away, and kept striding towards the ambulance. He had forgotten about design school. He had forgotten about the bud. He needed to get one last look at Mrs. Seltzer's oil drenched skin before they stored her away in some box or cubicle, far away from the swimming pool she loved so much.

DOG'S BREATH

THE DOG HAD been badly beaten. Maybe with a stick or a club with ragged edges. Hard to tell. Generally, I don't like dogs. They're dirty, have foul breath, and there's way too many of them running feral in the Red Deer valley. But this one was in rough shape. His ear had been cut off and his left eye punched out. Whoever had inflicted the savagery just tied the animal to a parking meter and left it there.

"That's not right," I said.

We were driving down Railway Avenue in my Dodge truck. Drumheller is a right-wing little prairie town dropped in the bottom of the Badlands like a coal mine in a crater. Chantal sat in the middle of the seat with a cold case of Pil on her lap. The condensation leaked in streams between her brown thighs and my pal Jackson sat on the far side watching the water disappear. Not tough to see where his head was at.

"What isn't?" she said.

I pulled the Dodge into a parking spot. When the tires hit the curb the steering wheel snapped out of my hand. Jackson bumped his head on the door frame and his Du Maurier spun into the ditch.

"Dude, what are you doing?" he said. He wasn't happy. We had picked Chantal up at the Dino Den and had an agreement in principle to head back to my place for a threesome.

"Stopping for the dog," I said.

"Are you out of your mind?" he said. "It's dead. It's been hit by a car."

"It's not dead. It's tied to the metre."

"Well, then it's got an owner and he'll be back."

"Why would someone leave a dog on the sidewalk?" I said.

"Who knows? Who cares?"

"My pants are getting wet," Chantal said.

"You heard the woman," Jackson said.

Jackson was technically right. Never lose the initiative if the woman's willing, and Chantal was predisposed. Along with the Pil we had a bag of weed and an entire Sunday afternoon to kill.

The poplar drooped in the August heat. A stream of pedestrians funneled around the doomed creature, none willing to stop. I shut the motor off.

"What are we supposed to do about this?" Jackson said.

"Pick it up, I guess."

"With what?"

"A shovel."

"What shovel?"

"I have a snow shovel in the flat bed."

"You're kidding me," he said.

"You can't touch a wounded animal," Chantal said. "It'll bite you. Hasn't anyone ever told you that?"

"Didn't your mother tell you that," Jackson said. "Better call her and get some remedial."

Jackson put his finger on Chantal's knee. The inside of the cab smelled of sweat and worn upholstery.

"Come on buddy," he said. "Let's go. Fuck the dog."

Jackson was the kind of guy I could do and not feel creepy about the next day, like you had to eat granola or show up at the Unitarian Church with him. His chest was always tanned and he wore beads along with a hippy sweater that gave him a Jim Morrison appeal. He never worked and spent most of the summer lying out on his lawn chair between the prickly pear cacti reading Faulkner, so you wouldn't guess what his inclinations were.

"We've got to take it somewhere," I said.

"Like where?"

"Like to the vet."

"We don't have time."

"It would take five minutes."

"It's Sunday. The vet is closed."

Rural Alberta. Pigs. Horses. Sheep. Sunday and the vet was closed.

"Then we'll take it to the emergency shelter."

"Buddy," Jackson said. "I hate to break this to you, but in my rear pocket I have got half an ounce of prime-time weed imported all the way from the beautiful socialist province of British Columbia and I don't fancy going anyplace except to your house to smoke it with this fabulous looking young blonde woman, and listen to your entire collection of Pink Floyd, nude."

The dog hyperventilated and his chest opened and closed like a bloodied accordion. It really was a pathetic creature, lanky, hair-less, and broken. An unruly cross between Doberman, Heeler and sausage, this was the stray that no one would want and I couldn't stand to watch it die in front of me.

Chantal shifted the crate of beer on her lap. "Can we go?" she said.

I got out of the truck and went around to the parking metre.

Terry, the owner of Terry's Family Tailor's that had held the same location since 1909, looked out through his plate glass window.

"Is the owner inside?" I said to him.

"I am the owner," he said.

"Of the dog."

Terry gazed at Chantal, my Dodge, Jackson, then dropped the venetian blinds on his shop.

"See what happens when you try and appease these people?" Jackson said.

The dog had no tag. The rope that secured him to the post was barn hemp, frazzled and covered with silt. I wondered if someone had dragged him out of the river. Every once in a while some oil rigger would get in shit for trying to drown his kittens in the river, but I don't think anyone had ever been charged. This isn't the kind of place where you charged people for killing animals.

The dog winced. His eye had been sealed up with railway tar. Almost like a ruffian medic had gone medieval on the wound. When I reached down to touch the mess, the ugly grey teeth snapped up in anger.

"Told you," Chantal said.

"Can you guys help me?" I said.

"I'm not getting out of the truck," she said. "It looks like I've pissed myself."

"Throw me a water bottle," I said.

"Why?" Jackson said. He leaned back in the seat and I knew where his hands were going.

"Its eye is infected."

"So what?" he said. "Now I suppose you want us to pick up some amoxicillin."

He fished around in the back seat and tossed me a bottle of club soda. I emptied the bottle onto the animal's eye and black chips washed out of the empty socket. Then I got the snow shovel from the box and pried the plastic blade under his spine. He howled, rolled over in pain, and shit himself.

Terry came out of his shop and wiped his hands on his apron.

"You're making a mess," he said.

"I'm helping the dog."

"You need to put money in the metre," he said.

When I had the dog wedged in between a spare tire and a flat of 10-40 weight, Jackson climbed out of the door, checked the arrangements of his love beads in the mirror, and ambled back to the bumper.

"I hate to interrupt your missionary work," he said. "But this is a once-in-a-lifetime opportunity and you are fucking it up supremely."

"We'll dump the dog in the backyard, give him a Tylenol, and then we can head inside," I said.

"Jesus," he said. "Please tell me you're still the horny bastard I've come to know and appreciate."

Well, he was right, I was. My dick was snarled up tight in the elastic band of my underwear and on the far side of the road a tumbleweed rolled off the sidewalk and across the centre line.

"Five minutes," I said.

Jackson chewed his lip and slapped me on the back.

We drove down Second Avenue past the Grain Exchange, the Presbyterian Church, and the hoodoos with the layers of grey sediment rising from the Red Deer River to the sky. The air smelled of petroleum.

"Do you have Pink Floyd?" Chantal said.

"Sure," I said.

"I love *Dark Side of the Moon* when I'm stoned. It gets me going."

"Tell me you have *Dark Side of the Moon*," Jackson said.

Chantal stared out the window and curled her finger around her blonde braid that had been tied to look like a wheat kernel. "You guys are into this, aren't you?"

"For most of my adult life," Jackson said.

"I mean, you won't jam out on me?"

"What makes you say that?" he said.

"I don't want a repeat of last week," she said. "Two guys from Linden. I picked them up at the Waldorf. That should have been my first clue. They said, oh yeah, we're flexible. We'll do anything. They wouldn't. Christ, they couldn't even get nude in the same room together."

"Linden," Jackson said. "Jesus. Don't worry about us."

She watched the parade of John Deere combines turn the corner and then her eyes flitted to the concrete Tyrannosaurus Rex that was filling up with tourists and monarch butterflies.

"I hate this place," she said.

"Why?" I said.

"It's like living on the inside of a toilet bowl. Except there's no water."

"There's the river," I said.

"It's a slough," she said. "Have you ever tried to swim in it? It's filled with fertilizer and green foam that makes your twat go numb. The moment you try and tan your tits the bylaw cops write you a pink for a hundred bucks. I've got three so far this summer."

"Did you pay them?" Jackson said.

"Not a chance," Chantal said.

She licked her index finger, rubbed it on my crotch, then slipped the diamond chipped nail into Jackson's mouth.

"Pinks will go to warrant," I said.

"How long have you guys been together?" she said.

"About twenty times," Jackson said, and I didn't realize it had been that many.

My bungalow sat at the end of an industrial road with crumpled sidewalks and railway ties strewn on the boulevard. I had a sagging porch, a screen door from the 1920s and a plastic swimming pool that was filled with weeds. Morally, I probably should have turned the house over to a better owner.

I parked the Dodge by the pool. Jackson and Chantal went straight inside. She perched herself on the kitchen counter, spread her legs, and jerked the toaster handle up and down like it was about to come. Jackson popped a Pil, yarded off his Grateful Dead shirt and did a rumba striptease for her.

It was twenty-nine degrees in the shade and probably forty-two in the sun. No place to leave a sick dog. The Badlands form a deep gulley that magnifies all the sunlight. Often bugs explode on the road and rattlesnakes bloat up in parking lots.

"Can we drink your JD?" she called out.

"Go ahead. It's in the..."

"Cupboard," Jackson said.

I got a potato sack and went to the truck. The dog was contorting either in the heat or the shame and I wrapped the burlap around his face so he couldn't bite me. He did anyway and ripped a long white gash into the back of my thumb. I couldn't figure out why the fucker hated me so much.

By the time I got inside, Chantal was supine over the toaster and Jackson was slurping JD out of her navel. As soon as the dog saw them, he spat white froth on the fridge.

"I'm just getting him an aspirin," I said. I put him down in the corner and got him a plate of water which he knocked over.

"Dogs can't eat aspirins," Chantal said from the hall. "It will kill them. It fries their liver."

"That's cats," I said. "Cats can't eat aspirins."

"Whatever," she said. She tugged on Jackson's hemp belt. The two of them were hip bumping in the living room. My living room is okay, I guess. It's by far the best room in the house on account of the floor doesn't sag, and there's one couch and this enormous picture window that stares out at an abandoned granary from World War II.

Jackson rolled a joint with Victory rolling papers. These ones were cherry flavoured with red maple leaves printed on them to make you feel patriotic when you lit up. Instantly the room filled with the stench of BC bud and my stomach went to knots.

"I'm going to Vancouver," Chantal said and took the joint from his hand. "Vancouver is really a fucking marvelous city. The cops don't hassle you if you light up a reefer there."

Chantal sucked in the weed and calculated the situation.

"The Floyd," she said. "Put on the Floyd."

My stereo, along with the Dodge, were my prized possessions. Not that it was all that good but I had owned it for twenty years and it came with monster black speakers that could still pound any jackhammer to shame. Like everything else in this valley it was a dinosaur that only a few appreciated. When the music made the window shake, Chantal sat back on the rattan chair and flicked off her shorts. The inside of her legs were a beautiful carmine colour and I just wanted to get my face stuffed in that sea of bitter bush.

"Strip for me, whore," she said. Her voice was suddenly hard and edgy so I figured the dope was catching up to her. She pointed at Jackson's crotch and made a downwards slash with her index finger.

Jackson stepped up to the plate and let his pants drop. He never wore underwear. His dick stuck straight out IBM missile style and Chantal rubbed her tits in semi circles with both palms.

At that moment my neighbours, Charles and Annette Benson, walked hand and hand down the street. He served in the Korean War, she was a nurse. They had a thing about railway spikes. No kidding, they collected them and had won some kind of historic prize. Something to do with their shape and dates, and they often took a field guide book along to identify the chunks of rusted metal.

"Who is that?" Jackson said. He downed the last bit of my JD then chased it with a beer.

"Neighbours," I said. "They collect railway spikes."

"I'll show them a spike," Jackson said. He went up to the window, which had no curtain, and swung his hips around so his cock oscillated like a wrecking bar. The Bensons looked up with half interest. It might have been too far away for them to see.

"Don't bother," I said.

"Why, it's your house isn't it?"

"They don't need to see that."

"Then they don't have to look."

"They can look at these," Chantal said. She went to the window and yarded off her top. Her nipples were pink, hard, and perfect globes. A work of art, really.

The Bensons gazed at the nubile set and then at me—not with shock, being vets and nurses and all, I don't think they got shocked a lot—and then they shuffled along with lacklustre acceptance.

"What a bunch of losers," Chantal said.

"Don't let them ruin the party," Jackson said.

"Get down and lick my feet," Chantal said and Jackson went for it, diving down to give her a tongue pedicure with his saliva soaking her instep.

"You too, bitch," Chantal said and gazed at me.

"As soon as I get the dog his Tylenol."

"Jesus," she said.

She grabbed Jackson by the hair and pulled him along on all fours towards the bedroom. He went willingly, panting and moaning worse than a donkey in heat.

The dog was curled up on a *Canadian Geographic* magazine by the fridge, hyperventilating. Every breath pained him. Every second that passed was one he didn't want and my kitchen was filled with the smell of a poorly kept kennel. I got a couple of Tylenol and crushed them up in Summer Sausage. He wolfed it down snarling at me all the time, the sick red gums sending out the fuck you message in dog language. I soaked a clean tea towel with salt water and sat down beside him. Off in the bedroom Jackson and Chantal stood facing each other stark naked. Two beautiful tanned bodies, a Bohemian monument to something, and all I had to do was just walk down with a tube of KY jelly and I could forget about the dog forever. I dribbled some water in the dog's eye and a stream of pus flooded out. Then the animal's face relaxed and his paws went limp like a great thistle had been taken from his soul. Just when I thought his one good eye was showing a splinter of compassion, he reared up and buried those diseased teeth into my groin and I fell over backwards knocking the Pil and car keys onto the shit-smeared linoleum floor.

GART'S GIRL

BRIAN AND SHELLEY were swingers. Everybody in town knew that. They had been married fourteen years and still went to the movies together, held hands, and did all the things that successful couples were supposed to do. On Sunday mornings they sat in the pink puffed booths of the Main Street Café and gave long accounts of the party they had held the previous evening.

Dale Rundle owned the café but didn't like the business much. He was a mechanic by trade and poured the coffee from too high up so it spattered onto the tables.

"Do you mind?" he said. "Can't you guys talk about anything but sex?"

"Um," Shelley said. She thought for a minute.

"The school board will be showing up and they order the full buffet. The last thing they want to hear about is your weekend wankings."

"Who's that?" Shelley said. She pointed with a fork to the other side of the café. A man with a hunting cap and a square face sat in front of a cup of coffee. He had the *Globe and Mail* opened, although it was obvious he wasn't reading anything.

"That's Gartner," Rundle said.

"He looks unhappy," Shelley said.

"His wife died a few months ago and he hasn't been the same since."

"What did she die of?"

"I'm not sure. It was leukemia or lupus or something that started with an L. The two of them used to come in here all the time. Now he just comes in by himself."

"Didn't recognize him," Shelly said.

"Well, I doubt he moves in your circles," Dale said. "He's probably got a family and entertains with his clothes on."

"Funny," Shelley said.

"You can never tell," Brian said. He picked a mayfly out of his coffee cup. "It could be your family we entertained last night."

"Don't creep me out, Brian," Rundle said. He shook his head and his neck shook too. "Sometimes he orders two coffees and I have to tell him he only needs one. Then he cries. I mean it's bad for business. When people are miserable like that, customers don't feel like eating."

"Don't be crass," Shelley said.

"Well then, you guys go and help him. You're supposed to be the ones who love everybody." Rundle held two fingers up like he was quoting the word.

Gartner stared at the paisley tablecloth. Every once in a while he flipped over a page from the newspaper, but the breeze from the kitchen flipped it back.

When Brian and Shelley were done, they didn't leave much of a tip for Rundle. He didn't move in their circles. They went out back to get their 1964 Ford Country Squire, which had a secret swinger symbol on the bumper, although everyone in town knew exactly what that meant, too.

They drove past the hardware store and stopped at the one and only traffic light in town. Dried thistle blew across the intersection. The air smelled of creosote.

"Isn't that Gartner sitting at the bus stop?" Brian said.

"I think so," Shelley said.

"Does the bus run on Sunday?"

"No," she said.

"What do you think we should do?"

She looked him over. "He's a handsome man."

Gartner stood up and gazed at something on the horizon, beyond the city water tower.

"Tall, too," she said. "Do you think Dera and Irene would like him?"

"What, the twins?" Brian said. "They'd eat him alive. Besides, they're longterm-ers. That's too heavy for a widower."

"How about Gwendolyn?"

"The blonde? The school teacher? Maybe."

The traffic light changed.

"We could give him a ride home," she said.

"Yeah, we could do that. Gwen reads the *Globe and Mail*."

Brian ran the Country Squire onto the curb and Shelley rolled down the window.

"Gartner?" she said. "It is Gartner, isn't it?"

Gartner waited a long time then turned towards the car. His face was a shattered windshield.

"Are you all right?" she said. "There's no bus today."

Garner didn't answer. Shelley and Brian glanced at each other once, then Brian put the wagon in park and they both got out.

"What are you looking at?" Brian said.

Gartner pointed at a landform that rose on the edge of town.

"I don't know what they're called," he said. "I forget my geography. The glaciers made them."

"Drumlins," Brian said. "They're called drumlins."

"Those," Gartner said.

The tear-shaped mounds rose a hundred feet from the prairie landscape and shimmered with durham wheat and the water tower couldn't hide them.

"They moved."

"What?" Brian said.

"I saw them."

"Okay," Brian said and glanced at his wife. "Let's get you home."

Shelley made a point of wrapping her arm around his waist. He smelled like lemon and they put him in the back seat of the wagon by a Rotortiller.

"He's got good abs," she said to her husband.

Gartner lived at the end of a Badland road in a small bungalow with a bird feeder out front. Inside, the furnishings were sparse and a stand-up clock was the only sound in the still air. The dining room table was set for two. Two plates, two coffee cups, two sets of cutlery, and a note in a woman's handwriting by the flower pot that said, "I love you." The oak table had been scrubbed with pine-scented cleaner and there were nine aerosol bottles discarded in the trash bin.

"I guess that's why he smells like he does," Shelley said.

Brian went into the bathroom and opened the medicine container. He pushed through a trough of Oxazepam, Prozac, and Trazodone. A round, pink pill bounced off the sink and rolled into the drain.

"Why don't we get you to bed?" Brian said.

They guided Gartner's crinkled frame to the bedroom and Brian kicked open the door. The room reeked of damp cotton. Women's clothes were scattered on the bed and dresser. There were three stacks of piano concertos that lay unsorted on the floor, and no room to walk.

"Do you think we should get the health nurse?" Shelley said.

Brian thought. "Not just yet. Do you have any one we can call, Gart? Anybody at all?"

"There's no one," he said.

After they had put him to bed they both stood at the doorway.

"We'll call you," Brian said.

"Maybe you'd like to come out with us sometime," Shelley said.

BRIAN AND SHELLEY went bowling on Monday mornings. Bowling was a thing people did on Monday morning if they hadn't had any luck on the weekend. Brachio Bowling was just off Railway Avenue. Half a dozen lanes of ten-pin and the same number of five-pin saw a lot of singles looking for someone to keep score for them. Brian and Shelley walked in with their ten-pin balls in leather travel cases. Gwen sat by herself at lane seven using an eraser on a score sheet. She watched the machine in lane six snatch the pins up and smoked with her mouth open like she'd just had an overdose of daytime TV.

"I thought her hair was blonde," Brian said.

"Last week," Shelley said.

Brian picked up three coffees with banana liquor in them at the counter. They admired the Robert Bateman print above the espresso machine then went over to Gwen's booth.

"Hey," she said.

"Hey."

"What are you doing here?"

Brian held up his sack. "We thought we'd throw a few frames. How was the marathon?"

Gwen shrugged. "I finished."

"That's something," Brian said and sipped the coffee. "I couldn't do that. I never would have finished. I can't even run down the block. Shelley always says to me, 'Brian, you've got to exercise more.'"

Gwen put down her pencil. In the hollow bowling cavern there were sounds of pins being knocked over and shoes sliding across smooth floors, and someone threw a gutter ball down in lane two. "How was your weekend?" she said.

Brian and Shelley shot each other the knowing glance. Sometimes they'd practice it at home in front of the mirror until they got the timing down right.

"Hot for September," Shelley said.

"Who was there?" Gwen said.

Brian touched the white rose that was pinned to his jacket lapel. The rose had the letter "S" on the petals. Safe. Sane. Secret. That was the rule.

"You know," he said.

Gwen stared off into space. She knew.

"This coffee is really terrible here," Shelley said.

"It's that time of year," Gwen said. "Everything tastes like mud."

"Why don't we go somewhere?" Brian said.

Gwen flexed the pencil between her fingers and scratched her ear with the eraser. The smell of burnt hot cross buns drifted over the counter, but it didn't cover up why people really came bowling on Monday. "There's not time."

"I meant, go somewhere to get some real coffee," Brian said. "Really?"

"Come on, we'll buy. Rundle's. I didn't feel like bowling anyway."

Gwen gazed down at the scorecard. There was her name and someone else's. A Gary F. "I've got a ten o'clock blind bowl."

"Who's Gary F?"

"Obviously a flunkie because it's five after eleven."

"That's too bad," Shelley said.

"I don't know why I even bother coming here."

"Someone was asking about you this weekend," Brian said.

A bunch of pins got knocked over in lane two. Someone screamed like they'd witnessed a car crash. For a long time the automatic pick-up machine hovered over the pins unable to decide what to do.

"Let's go," Gwen said.

OUTSIDE, BRIAN FIGURED Gwen looked a lot better in the sun. Cowboy boots, tight jeans. Girls who wore cowboy boots in the autumn always looked good. Like they were fit for the Stampede even in the winter. He opened the door to Rundle's and listened to the bell dingle above Gwen's head. The café was deserted. There was a smell of sage in the room.

"So how was the marathon after-party?" Brian said.

"There wasn't one."

"I thought that was the point."

They sat down at the table beside the window. No sign of Gartner. The special was apple bacon and Triassic fries. "People's feet are cramping up. They're dehydrated and there's so many intestinal knots, nobody is in the mood."

"Super."

Rundle came out of the back room with a broom and dust pan. He was also wearing his clean-up apron, which was bad news. The apron was pink and whenever Rundle had it on it meant there'd been some kind of calamity in the kitchen.

"What are you guys doing in here?" he said.

"We're customers," Shelley said. "You own a café and we'd like some café au lait."

"It'll have to wait."

"Why?"

"We've had a dirt storm. The café is closed."

"The OPEN sign is still up."

"It shouldn't be."

Brian glanced around. The floor of the café was covered in a thin film of silt. The floor, the tables, the chairs. It made the café look pastel, and not very clean. There were bits of cactus mixed in with the dust.

Gwen ran her finger over the tablecloth. "It's clay. Not dirt. Aeolian transport. Eventually it can form dunes." She held a tiny shell fossil up to the window light.

"You and Gart will get on good," Brian said. "He's into all that science stuff."

"Gart?" she said. She put the trilobite down on the napkin.

"You know Gartner. He owned the gas station. Remember?"

Gwen lifted her index finger and placed it on her lip. From somewhere deep in the past a memory surfaced. Outside, the birch were yellow and drooping in drought. She rolled the fossil between her fingers.

"Yep," Shelley said. "That one."

"Isn't he married?"

"Was. He's a widower. Has been for a while."

"Forget it, then," she said.

"No, a long while. Don't sweat it. He's back in the loop."

Rundle went to the door and flipped over the OPEN sign so it read CLOSED. Then he came back to the table. His brow was damp and he looked like his cat had just died. "I'm sorry, I can't serve anyone now."

"Why not?" Brian said.

"Because of all this sand. Why doesn't the city plant more trees on the boulevard? Isn't that what you socialists do, plant trees?"

"I don't care about the clay," Shelley said.

"The health inspector might."

"But you look so good cleaning up in that apron."

"Knock it off."

When Rundle went to the back room to get a dustpan, Brian got up and walked over to the coffee machine. That was the great thing about Rundle. He'd tell customers he couldn't serve them because of some geophysical calamity, then forget about it. Brian poured out three cups of the Guatemalan blend and they all sat down at a table.

"What's this Gart fellow into?" Gwen said.

Some people liked swinging in the autumn because it was hot. Other people liked swinging in the autumn because it made them melancholy and do things they wouldn't otherwise dream of. The best kind were the people who put it off all summer for reasons they wouldn't admit to and, come September, desires would crash back with a vengeance. Those ones would do anything.

"You name it," Brian said.

"I want a guy I can really work over," Gwen said. She leaned back in the chair and flipped out a package of menthol cigarettes, and then she owned the morning.

"He's your man."

"He's not 10-21 is he?" 10-21 was the code the cops used in Calgary to mean mental case. "The widow part I can deal with, but I can't stand the crazy ones."

"He's owned his own business for eleven years."

"You seem keen on him."

"We just want to help out our neighbours."

Gwen turned her cigarette over. She ran the fossil through the dirt and made a small letter G in the silt.

GARTNER SHOWED UP in a suit because he didn't know what to wear to these kinds of parties. Brian and Shelley lived in a brick rancher left over from the seventies. The porch sagged in the middle and there was a mountain ash in the centre of the lawn. When Brian answered the door he saw Gart had that look on his face that said he just wanted to go home, which was bad, but also an expression of desperation, like he'd spent half an hour preparing his tie in front of the mirror, which was good. The tie was black but had an orange owl peeking out from a birch tree.

"Come on in," Brian said and pushed the screen open. Brian was wearing a tie too, but he also had on jeans and sneakers.

Inside the small living room there were three other couples and a single woman in a pink nylon suit drinking tonic on a rattan chair. Wagner was playing on the stereo and a white cat slept on a Persian rug.

"You're all dressed up," Shelley said. She stood up and came over and threw her arms around him. She was wearing cashmere and smelled of fruit perfume.

"I didn't know what to wear," he said.

"Don't worry about us," Brian said. "We're pretty casual here. We don't care what you wear."

"Or if you wear anything at all," Shelley said. She took the tie out of his suit and waved it between two fingers. "Isn't he hot? Oh my god, look at this tie. Isn't he hot?"

"He's hot," the blonde woman on the couch said. She put her foot on the knee of a well-built man with red hair. Brian knew him as a firefighter but wasn't about to bring up vocations yet.

"Come on in and sit down," Brian said. "Do you want a drink?"

"I probably shouldn't."

"Come on. Last weekend of summer, technically."

"I'll mix it light," Brian said.

"I'll hand it to you," Gwen said. She leaned against the kitchen wall and stirred her gin with a pink swizzle stick. She looked him over and tucked the stick in the corner of her mouth. The room got hot and damp and for a moment the only sounds were Brian and Shelley breathing.

"Okay," Gart said.

"I'm Gwen," she said, shook his hand, and they sat down on the couch together. She didn't even have to mix the drink because Brian had already done that.

"People call me Gart," he said.

"What do you do?" she asked. "I mean for a living?"

"I used to run the gas station on the corner of Highway Nine."

"I remember. The one with the glass dome in the top that the fuel ran through."

"That's the one."

"I liked that. I mean for some reason I liked the idea of being able to see what was going into my car. Isn't that weird?"

"No, that's not weird," Gartner said. "That's the reason I did it."

"Really. Do you still have it? The gas station, I mean."

"No." He looked down. "It's been closed for a few months now."

"Oh," Gwen said, but didn't ask why.

"We're listening to Wagner," Brian said. "We don't know much about him. This is one of those Best of the Classics albums and it sounds better loud."

"This is 'Flight of the Valkyries,'" Gartner said.

"You know classics?" Shelley said.

"A bit."

"I read somewhere that he was an anti-Semite," the firefighter said, and looked worried.

"Anti-Semite?" Brian whistled. "Do you know anything about that, Gart?"

"I just know it was good to pump gas to," Gartner said. "The idea that petrified plants could be turned into pistons exploding appealed to me."

"That's a good one," the firefighter said.

Gwen put her index finger between her teeth. Her nails were painted a bright red and had small diamonds indented in the tips.

"Were you at Alfie's party last week?" Shelley said.

"They're into that bubble-n-tubble stuff, aren't they?" Brian asked.

"Mm," Gwen said.

"We're not really into that stuff much," Brian said. "I mean, *suum cuique.* But I pretty much want to make things happen on time."

"Are you into it?" Gwen said. She rested a hand on Gartner's chest.

The room waited for an answer. The firefighter flexed his enormously muscular biceps and the brunette standing by the television pulled down on her T-shirt.

"I'm not sure," he said. "My wife and I were pretty conventional."

"What's conventional?"

"We didn't do much." Gartner stared out the window and sipped scotch out of the crystal tumbler. Down the narrow town road, the aspens bent over the crumpled pavement in a canopy of green and the evening smelled of lawn trimmings. "I mean, I guess we should have, you know. Now that I think about it, we should have done more." Gartner sat and stared down at his glass. The ice popped and shrank. His jaw quivered. "We move like drumlins, our species."

The Wagner finished. The cat rolled over. Down the block, a cement mixer emptied its load.

"Tell me about the drumlins," Gwen said. She bit down on one of her crimson fingernails.

"You'd think I'm crazy."

"Tell me about how they moved, Gart."

Brian felt a hot autumn breeze blow through the open window. Gwen had let her hand fall between her thighs. She wasn't wearing underwear. There was a mole. She had on red fishnet stockings and she was talking about glacial landforms and she wasn't wearing any underwear.

"I'm sorry," Gartner said. He stood up and straightened his

tie. "I shouldn't have come. I've ruined your party. I apologize. I know you all want to have a good time and you're very nice people. Maybe some time I'll be able to come again, but not tonight."

"Listen, I tell you what, Gartner," Brian said. He stood up. "We can't let you go just yet. We'd feel bad. Have at least one drink with us. Stay five minutes. Laugh once. Gwen and Shelley do this great routine where they dress up in wet newsprint pages and we have to guess what paper they're from. I'll bet you're a *Globe and Mail* kind of guy."

"I'll let you read the editorial page," Gwen said.

Brian clinked his glass against Gart's scotch. It was cold and shards of ice crept down the side of the glass. Beautiful, beckoning beacons of party promise. So when Brian made a treaty invitation to his guest and Gart smiled for the first time, it made him feel bold and optimistic, like he was standing on the edge of a vast new continent.

A LOT LATER in the evening, when the sky was black and a cool wind blew down off the prairie, the only sound was the spray of rotating sprinklers across lawns. Brian picked out the last beer from the ice chest and walked through his living room. He liked how still the house was after a party and how absolutely harboured they were from the prejudice of their awkward valley. Perhaps a million years of sediment had cemented everything in the right place. The firefighter had gone to sleep on the couch. There was a woman's fishnet bodysuit on the floor by the television and the cat was sleeping on the sleeve.

Brian went outside. He closed the door. Far above him the stars were small and bright and he knew the night could get cold if it wanted to, and then he smelled a menthol cigarette. Gwen was sitting on the bench beneath the clothesline with her back against the stucco. She still had on her leather bra and halter shorts, but her feet were bare. She gazed up into the stars and exhaled.

"That was quite the party, Brian."

"I'm glad you enjoyed yourself."

"Did you?"

Brian sat down on the bench beside Gwen. A beautiful mixture of sweat and perfume rolled off her shoulders. He tugged her once on the earlobe and didn't have to answer.

Gwen nodded. She flicked some ashes onto the lawn and rolled her tongue between her lip and top teeth. Far off in the distance a drone of cicadas or grasshoppers—Brian could never tell which—continued with their nightly sermon.

"I think I hurt him," she said.

"Who?"

"Gart."

"Which part?"

"Right at the end."

"Oh, that," Brian said. He patted her thigh.

"He cried."

"Big boys cry all the time."

A moth fluttered around the light on the tool shed. Gwen looked like she was trying to say something, but somehow the words just wouldn't come out, and then a meteorite slid across the sky.

"Don't sweat it."

"I am."

"You can't tell me that you haven't hurt a man before. Just look up at the heavens. Everything is in its place. What a beautiful evening. I can't remember if it's this weekend or next when the auroras start."

This was the moment when Gwen was supposed to roll her eyes, laugh, and get all dreamy. Or praise Brian for mixing the drinks too strong, or say, "there's a thin line between pleasure and pain." But she didn't. She just turned the cigarette between her thumb and finger and looked like she was trying to articulate the difference between a deciduous and coniferous forest.

"I meant afterwards," she said.

"After?"

"You weren't watching then. Everyone figured the show was over. He cried. He told me his wife had always been a person of reason, the type who liked balancing equations and making sense of things. She owned a theodolite and was a surveyor by trade. Then he told me he still loved her and he thought what he had done was wrong."

"He loved it."

"You get this look in your eyes like a predatory bird."

"Survival of the fittest."

"Whatever."

"I'll talk to him."

"He left."

"Left?"

"Out the door. In fact, he left in so much of a hurry, he forgot his tie."

Gwen held up the tie. The orange owl was crumpled and lost in silk caverns. Brian slipped the tie out of her fingers and rolled it through his palm. This wasn't good news. A widowed man who saw lumps of dirt move and liked confessing party secrets to strangers wandering the streets wasn't good news at all. Brian gazed out to a

Russian olive grove from where anything could spring: a bear, a flood, or simply the unknown thistle from the worst place in your neighbourhood.

Inside the Country Squire the air smelled of a foreign perfume, which was not odd: the Squire often smelled of strangers after parties, but Brian was not comforted. He turned on the heater but all the vent did was to blow more cold air around.

There would not be many people on the streets this time of night, so anything that moved would probably be Gartner. He would be the one with ruffled hair and no tie muttering about Miocene landforms or ketamine dosage. Brian drove past Gartner's house and the gas station where nothing breathed, so he rolled onto Main Street and saw the single light of Rundle's Café blaring through the dark.

The café was filled with harsh white and yellow hues and checkered tablecloths that were too brash for three in the morning. There were chrome toasters and cheap china plates and all the unfriendly things that were supposed to be in sterile main street cafes. But in the corner table sat two people huddled together awaiting some grave news. Gartner had his head down on a napkin and his palms on top of his scalp. His shirt buttons were still undone and even from outside the door there was the awkward sound of a man sobbing. Rundle sat in his pink apron leaning forward with his knuckles pushed into his jaw. Brian had seen people look like this on an old newscast when they stared into a radio and listened to the Prime Minister declare war.

He sucked in a breath and opened the glass door. The bell jingled above his head. Gartner did not move, but Rundle turned around and put one hand on his knee.

"What the hell do you want?" he said.

"Hey, hey, I just came by to see if our favourite house guest has been located."

"He's here."

Brian waltzed between two tables and picked up a soup spoon to see if there was still any dust on it.

"That's great. Some of our guests got worried. Guess Gart had quite a bit to drink."

Rundle stood up and his fists shook and the fat on his neck shook again too. "You're a real asshole, you know, Brian," he said. He rolled up his left sleeve and then his right one and this frightened Brian, because although he had heard of people rolling up their sleeves, he had never really seen the act unfold. "You and your goddamn friends. If I had my way I'd tie you up and leave you on the road all banged up, but that would make me as bad as you, so I won't. But I can still toss you out of my own café in a way you won't forget."

Rundle's pace gathered locomotive steam, heavy and black, burgeoning down the tracks. And as the last few inches closed between the two men, Brian thought of how absolutely and exquisitely good human beings could be one moment and yet, in the next, so much the other thing.

WHAT GOOD FRIENDS DO

WE MOVED TO the valley a year ago to get away from the stress. I raised bees and Fran kilned pots. Not that we made a lot of money. Money wasn't the point. We needed a place where you didn't worry about your blood pressure or care what other people said behind your back. But raising bees wasn't as easy as I thought. They got mites, the neighbours bitched, and there wasn't a lot of cash in them, so I got looking for a part-time job.

A friend of mine, Harold, who'd I'd met at a civil liberties meeting, was a shop steward at the brewery. He said he could get me work one day a week. That was all I needed. Harold was keen on me because I raised bees.

"Why don't you and Fran come on over for dinner?" he said. "We can have a couple of beer and talk things out."

Sure, I said. What the hell. Beer and steak. Might be fun. Fran needed a little more convincing.

"I don't like the sounds of that," she said. She sat at the kitchen table and stared at the yellowed linoleum that needed to be replaced.

"What's not to like?"

"What do they want?"

"I guess just to have dinner with us."

"They probably want to have sex with us."

"What?" I put a jar of honey down on the counter.

"You made it sound like he's checking you out."

"For the job, Fran."

"Couldn't he do that at the meetings?"

Fran didn't go to meetings. That's one of the reasons we left Calgary.

"Maybe it's a conflict of interest," I said.

She stood up like she was going to give a speech, but knocked over the cutlery pot instead. The spoons rattled on the floor. "Jesus," she said. "How did that happen?"

Fran spent a lot of time in the bathroom getting her makeup on. She was usually a quick dresser. So I had no idea what was going on. I didn't mind. Fran always looked good. Especially for tennis. I wasn't ready for what came out the door. Crimson lipstick, pink mini skirt, and five-inch heels.

"What's this?" I said.

"You wanted me to look nice."

"You look nice all the time."

"Getting this job is important."

"You didn't have to dress up."

"We need new linoleum," she said.

I went out and started the car. The seat had to be brushed off because Fran didn't want fur on her skirt. Some kind of animal had taken up nocturnal residence in our Toyota and left hair on the upholstery. No matter how tight I locked up the barn, the dirty creature got in every night and left fuzz on the headrests.

"You've got to do something about that beast," she said.

"It's clean now."

She got her Miracle Brush that she purchased off the adver-
tizing station at four a.m. and combed the seat again. After the
fur had been chucked in the incinerator, I drove down River
Avenue, past the fossil shop, and crossed into town. Fran stared
ahead into the crimson sunset and clutched her purse. She
bowled a bunch of filthy words around in her mouth, and when
the two globes of the purse lock wouldn't stay shut, she pitched it
onto the dash.

"Stop at the liquor store," she said.

"What do you want?"

"BC Chardonnay. You know the kind I like. Burrowing Fowl."

"Owl?"

"Get some."

I pulled the car into the parking lot. Asking for BC wine in the
black heart of petroleum country was like trying to hawk a k.d.
lang album at an abattoir. There was a couple off the blood reserve
in a Ford truck beside us. They had an Old Glory flag stuck in their
rear window, which didn't make a lot of sense to me, but they
appreciated Fran's dress.

"Can't we park somewhere else?" Fran said.

"Why?"

"They're scaring me."

"What's wrong?"

Fran managed to scour a twenty out of the bottom of her purse.
"Forget the wine. Get me some Smirnoff, no wait, Canadian Club.
A twenty-sixer of cc."

I figured we could take a cab home if we had to.

"Do you have any pot?"

"I don't have any pot."

I didn't have anything against pot. I graduated from university. Fran thought weed calmed her down, but it didn't. It made her hyper and then she'd eat Styrofoam.

"Do you think Harold and Bonnie will have any?" she said.

"It's not something you ask on the first date."

"Why not?"

"He's the chapter member of the Alberta Civil Liberties Society. You'll be fine."

But as soon as we started walking up the steps to Harold's place, I knew it wasn't going to be fine. Fran's teeth chattered and white pith clung to her lips. She put one arm on the mailbox and sucked in air to stay standing. Harold opened the door and held up both hands. He was a big solid man, six feet and two hundred easy, but he was like a giant Ukrainian teddy bear. The kind of guy who volunteered for charities and still enjoyed a gallon of vodka by the fire.

"Hey buddy," he said. "Come on in here, you two. Winter's a coming. Get in here."

They had a rancher with polished wood floors and a marble fireplace. The kitchen smelled like baking bread and there was a photo of Pierre Trudeau above the mantel.

"Bonnie, our guests are here," he called out. "Break out the booze. Put your clothes back on."

A woman in a blue chiffon dress glided out of a fifties daytime series and into the room. Her feet didn't seem to move as she swept across the floor.

"Well howdy, you two," she said and put one fist on her hip.

"I've heard so much about you," Harold said. He gave Fran a friendly once over. "About how you brought this guy over onto the side of common sense and freedom."

"It was an accident," Fran said.

We all laughed. Fran sort of laughed too but her jaw trembled.

"And I've heard so much about you, Harold," she said. "About how at the ACLA meetings you two would go into the back room and give each other blow jobs. Then you'd screw each other hard, hard in the ass, you dick-licking homos."

An ice pick froze the room. Outside the window a goldfinch fluttered from branch to branch. Fran had a grin pasted to her face like she'd said something smart and was expecting a compliment.

"Pardon?" Harold said.

The second was misty blue and the future might have been interpreted. But the second passed and Fran's face cracked into crystals on a winter pond. She made a bullfrog sound then darted for the door. On the way down the steps her heel twisted into a crack and snapped the stiletto. She crawled on all fours to the Toyota and slithered onto the passenger seat.

BACK AT THE house, I put ice on Fran's ankle. Mascara ran in lines down her face.

"Do you want some aspirin?"

"No."

"It was a slip of the tongue," I said. "These things happen."

She bit down on her knuckle. "I knew it was coming."

"How?"

"I'd been rehearsing the lines in the car."

"For ten miles?"

Outside, one of my bees bumped into the window then flew off as if the collision hadn't made any sense to him.

"I don't want to see either of those people again as long as I live," she said.

"It's a small town, Fran. You're going to see them again."

"I'll stay inside."

"You can't do that."

"Watch me."

"How about we go and see the doctor?"

Fran lifted her head out of the pillow and stared at me incredulously. "A doctor? I don't need a doctor. It's this stupid town that's driving me crazy with its hillbillies and redneck dinosaurs. I don't need a doctor, I need an exorcist."

The next morning I made an appointment with the walk-in clinic anyway. A doctor Habowitz would see her at nine, but the nurse stressed that if Fran didn't want to come in there was no way to force her. After I'd made the appointment I told Fran what I'd done. She didn't take it badly, just another event that had to be processed, like a dentist appointment or divorce papers.

Fran didn't want me inside the room with the doctor, which worried me. Still, I figured we'd made a promising first step, which is better than what happens with most couples when one of them has to see a shrink. After twenty minutes she came out of the room with a business grin on her face and a prescription between two fingers. She said goodbye to the doctor and he waved at me. I waited until we were away from the clinic on our way to the pharmacy.

"Well?" I said.

"Not too much to report."

"What did he say?"

"That it was most likely stress caused by the move and he gave me a prescription for Ativan. He said if it hasn't improved in seven days to come right back and see him, and he says next time he'll talk to you too."

"What did you tell him?"

"I told him I'd been feeling displaced about finances and country living and that for some reason unknown I spewed off a list of profanities when we went out for dinner at a friend's place."

"You told him word for word what you said?"

"Yes."

"What did he think?"

"He wanted to know if you had any latent homosexual desires and if I felt that posed a threat to my femininity."

"What did you say to that?"

Fran didn't answer that question. She slipped the prescription into her purse and snapped it shut. This time the snaps worked.

"Have you noticed that there seems to be a disproportionate number of transsexuals in this town?" she said. We walked under a neon arch that advertized gasoline in both litres and gallons. "I mean for its size. In a relative sense. Naturally there wouldn't be as many here as Vancouver or New York, but this is a smaller place. They are everywhere here, especially in the morning. I don't know what percentage of men are into that kind of thing. Say, one percent. In a town of five thousand that means there would only be twenty-five at the most, given an equal gender division. And most of those would never be seen in public. But here, you see them everywhere."

"Where?"

"That one right there." Fran pointed into the Petro-Can parking lot where a pretty girl in a halter top was pumping unleaded into her Volkswagen.

"She's not a transsexual."

"How can you tell?"

"Because she's not. Look at her. She's got hips."

"So you are an expert? Don't stare at him. That's rude."

"It's not a he."

We cut through the gas station island. Mostly young people filled up at Petro-Can. The old folks didn't like it because they thought it had something to do with socialism, and a lot of people had bumper stickers that said "I'd rather push this truck a mile than buy from Petro-Can." The young one was cute. Full lips, long legs. If he was a transsexual, she had me fooled.

"Morning," I said.

"Morning," the girl said and looked up from her pump. She sized me and Fran up and smiled. Then she readjusted her jeans and went back to her gas.

"Told you," I said.

"I want steak for dinner. The doctor said along with the Ativan I have to eat right and he said, just by looking at me, I wasn't doing that."

He was probably right there. Fran had lost weight. I'd been trying to put honey on her toast in the morning but she wouldn't have anything to do with that. We went into the grocery store and the air was cool. I never liked grocery shopping and as soon as Fran wheeled out the cart my mind started to drift. I thought about bees and the monster that was living in our car. And then I thought about the girl at the gas pump. I thought about her dropping her halter top and about Harold and Bonnie showing up.

"Sirloin or tenderloin?" Fran said to me. She had a package in each hand.

"Uh?"

"If you're not going to help I'm going to buy both and then when the Visa bill comes in you can figure it out."

I went up to the till feeling gloomy. Events were going down-hill and I couldn't figure out how to reverse them.

"Barbecue tonight?" the clerk said. He was a middle-aged man who looked like he had Greek in him and enjoyed his job. Behind him stood a teenage girl with freckles who was bagging the groceries. She wanted to give away paper coupons.

"You bet," Fran said. "We're going to have both the tender- · loin and the sirloin."

"What kind of sauce?" said the clerk.

"Teriyaki," she said. "I make it myself."

"That's great."

"And we grow our own mushrooms in the backyard. You're only supposed to be able to grow them in Vancouver, but my husband has a greenhouse so we grow them here all year."

"Super."

"And then do you know what I'm going to do?" Fran said.

"No, what?" the clerk said.

"I'm going to take off all of my clothes and hang myself. It's the asphyxia thing. I'm going to wrap a rope around my neck, get my vibrator and hang myself until I come. If my husband doesn't cut me down in time, I'll be dead, so if I'm not shopping tomorrow, call the police. Our house is the one with all the bees in the back and the shitty linoleum on the floor."

The girl put down her sack of groceries and bit her finger. In a second we were outside in the bright sun. Fran walked awk-wardly, as if in a trance.

FRAN WAS ASLEEP and I went out to tend to the bees. I had a dozen stacks of mellifera mellifera in the middle of a clover field and sometimes I stood there in my white suit with the buzzing all around because it calmed me. From far on the other side of the clover patch a bee-suited figure strode towards me. I'd never seen that before. Someone else in a suit. I'd always done the bees by myself. Whoever was inside didn't look very comfortable, like they couldn't make the shoulders fit right. My visitor tripped in a gopher hole and I thought for a second it was Fran. I couldn't decide if that would be good or bad.

"Hey, buddy," the man behind the net said. "Listen, I'm sorry for pilfering the suit. I tried to call you from the barn. I was scared to come out here unarmed."

"Harold?"

"The same." Harold readjusted the net over his face. His belly split the fabric and the cuffs hung on his elbow. "I couldn't leave this any longer but these bees just creep me out so I hope you don't mind. I didn't disturb any kind of protocol, did I?"

"I'm glad you came."

"Me too. Hey, have you ever tried honey beer? It's from Switzerland and made from bees."

"No."

"How is Fran?"

"Not good."

"I'm sorry to hear that."

"Look, I'm really sorry about last time."

Harold picked at some clover. "How is she this time?"

I put down my smoke pot. Up on the prairie someone batted a ball around on a tennis court.

"This time?"

"That's kind of why I'm here, buddy. Can we walk away from these hives?" Harold held me by the elbow as we made our way over the potholed field back to the house. "This is a small town. Everybody knows everybody. Everybody talks. Pick your friends carefully. Know your parties, if you get my drift. Eddy from the grocery store called me and he was furious. I guess what Fran said at the checkout didn't go over so well. The clerk's assistant was only seventeen. Anyway, Eddy called me on account of my position and he said, 'Is that legal, can she say those kinds of things? Is it in the Constitution or what?' Buddy, I covered for you. I said you were my friends and that Fran was stressed. He said do something about it by noon or he'll go to the cops. I've been trying to find you all morning."

I looked at my watch. "What does he want you to do?"

"Just to call him and let him know your wife isn't a pedophile."

I unlocked the barn and slid off the padlock. Thunder came down. A dog barked, and inside, a square bale of hay had been put through a shredder and spat on the walls.

"Are you expecting burglars?" Harold said.

"Animal problems."

The phone was one of those old wall phones on the centre post and Harold went straight for the dial. Then he stood with the receiver in his hand and gazed into the car. The upholstery had been ripped into long shreds. There was matted fur on the steering wheel and feces smeared on the window.

"Some animal," he said.

"It rips the upholstery up," I said. "Pillows, clothes. Havana cigars. Last week it chewed all my Irving Klaw magazines to bits."

"That's crazy."

"We came out here for peace and quiet. The last thing we need is a Tasmanian devil tearing into our personal lives."

Harold nodded. Something was on his mind. He stuck a finger in the dial and rung up Eddy. He turned away from me and
leaned against the post. "Eddy," he said. "Harold here. Listen, I
just had a word with Fran's husband. No pedophilia. It's these
bees. She's seeing a doctor. Something like Tourette's."

Then he mumbled in a low, slow voice with his hand over the
phone, and so I opened the car door and climbed inside. Things were
worse than I had thought. The critter had pissed all over the back
seat. Cat urine and pickle juice do the very worst on your mortgage
rate. Another bucket-seat would cost two hundred dollars easy.

"Buddy," Harold said and slapped me on the back. "It's all
patched over."

"The doc has got her on Ativan now so maybe that will help
things out."

"You look like you could use one."

"He gave her exactly fourteen. She'd notice if any were missing."

"Well," he said. "I do have something that might help."

I didn't have to think for too long. The past was the past. I needed
a future.

"That a boy, bud."

Harold pulled out what looked like a cellphone. He flipped a
switch and the case opened. Five thinly rolled joints were
crammed inside. Harold told me that they were homegrown and
had something to do with the way the Horseshoe Canyon reflected
the light on chernozemic soil. We passed the weed back and forth
and the barn filled up with green smoke. I started laughing even
though nothing was funny. Then an odd feeling crept into me. I
started thinking about Bonnie stepping out of her chiffon dress
and orgies at the Tyrell Museum and reptilian critters breaking

into my house. The phone rang and I hit my head on a rafter. Harold spent the next two rings stamping out the roach that had long since died on the dirt floor.

Harold picked up the phone. He was breathing heavy. His eyes were white and round as if he were receiving the news of a nuclear explosion. Someone on the other end was shouting.

"Fran is at Rundle's Café," he said. "She's throwing plates at the window."

"She's in our bedroom sleeping."

"She's taking her clothes off. Eddy says she's got a tattoo of a dragon on her belly."

Vancouver, 1993. The Smiling Buddha. David Suzuki had just given a lecture at the university. We'd been happy then.

Rundle's Café had pretty much cleared out by the time we got there. Rundle was standing back behind the till clenching a broom with both hands. Generally Rundle's was kind of a conservative throwback to the fifties, where you could take your kids, talk about the British monarchy, and get run of the mill black coffee with eggs.

Fran was up on the table. Her face stretched into lava flows but her mouth was angular and sharp. I would not have recognized her except for the tattoo. She didn't acknowledge my existence. She made a fist and yelled at the chandelier.

"I've called the cops," Rundle said.

"I would advise we take care of this long before the police show up," Harold said.

I went over to the table. Fran kicked off the cutlery. There were a couple of plates that were smashed too. She had put on her five inch stilettos again. I held out my hands. Her eyes flitted my way. Except they weren't her eyes anymore. They were unfocussed like a coyote run over by a truck.

"Do you know what this animal did?" she said. Her finger curled around what was left of her belt and she addressed the empty room. "He killed our children. He tortured our only child and he sodomized her for months in our basement, and then he burned the body so no one would catch him."

Fran picked up the napkin holder and pitched it at the window. "I'll pay for it," I said to Rundle.

"It's not the napkin holder I'm worried about," Rundle said. He pointed a soup ladle at the far wall.

The far wall had been ripped like a Rotortiller had been driven through the plaster. Maybe it was the dope. Maybe it was just lack of compassion. Maybe it was the smartest thing to do. I reached up and snagged Fran's arm. The table gave way and I felt the cartilage in her wrist crack. Before she had a chance to stand I had her in a half nelson and she kicked me in the balls. Harold did a calculation, gritted his teeth, and wrapped his huge arms around Fran's knees. Outside it was a beautiful autumn day. I guess that's one of the reasons we loved the place so much: the red maples, the cottonwood and crimson cherry trees. Problem was, a lot of other people liked it too, and they were all out on the street, wandering up and down this quaint, little pre-war town looking in shop windows or else meeting friends and talking about wheat prices. Two men in white bee suits were dragging a screaming woman down Main Street towards an unknown future. A few people talked on their cellphones. Someone took a photo. No one intervened. When the barn came into sight, Fran seized the collar of Harold's bee suit.

"Not in there," she said. "That thing lives in there. Harold, listen to me. My husband is a demon and he wants to kill us. Please, God, let us go back to where we belong."

Either the collar of the bee suit distracted Harold or else what Fran had said caught him off guard. He lost his grip and she bit his hand. There was blood and breaking of fingers. Fran ran away past the barn. She kept on going towards the beehives where the swarm of creatures waited. The very creatures that would eventually envelop her, the valley, and maybe in the end, all of us, too.

ABOUT THE AUTHOR

Martin West was born in Victoria and spent his youth drifting throughout BC, the Yukon, and Alberta. He graduated from the University of British Columbia and his stories have been published in magazines across the nation and twice included in the Journey Prize Anthology.